"Do you want to take her?" Martha asked, and Lewis instantly looked alarmed.

"Don't panic, there's no nappy changing required! Just give her a bit of a cuddle."

Lewis did his best, but the fact was that Viola wasn't the slightest bit interested. It was more fun to explore her uncle's face with inquisitive little fingers, sticking them in his mouth, patting his nose, tugging at his lips and pulling at his hair until he winced.

"Why won't she sit quietly like him?" Lewis complained, casting an envious glance to where Noah was sitting angelically on his mother's lap.

"Just wait until she's old enough to answer back!"

"That'll be her parents' problem," said Lewis, removing Viola's finger from his ear. "It's nothing to do with me."

Even to himself that had the ring of famous last words.

What happens when you suddenly discover your happy twosome is about to be turned into a...*family?*

Do you panic?

Do you laugh?

Do you cry?

Or...do you get married?

The answer is all of the above—and plenty more!

Share the laughter and the tears as these unsuspecting couples are plunged into parenthood! Whether it's a baby on the way or the creation of a brand-new instant family, these men and women have no choice but to be

READY FOR BABY!

When parenthood takes you by surprise!

Look out for the next book in the Ready for Baby miniseries, *The Pregnant Tycoon* by Caroline Anderson— coming in July 2004 in Harlequin Romance®!

If you'd like to find out more about Jessica Hart, you can visit her Web site
www.jessicahart.co.uk

HER BOSS'S
BABY PLAN
Jessica Hart

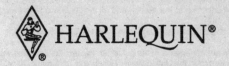

TORONTO • NEW YORK • LONDON
AMSTERDAM • PARIS • SYDNEY • HAMBURG
STOCKHOLM • ATHENS • TOKYO • MILAN • MADRID
PRAGUE • WARSAW • BUDAPEST • AUCKLAND

For Dora, with love

ISBN 0-373-03797-X

HER BOSS'S BABY PLAN

First North American Publication 2004.

Copyright © 2003 by Jessica Hart.

CHAPTER ONE

MARTHA looked at her watch. Twenty to four. How much longer was Lewis Mansfield going to keep her waiting?

His PA had apologised when she had turned up as instructed at three o'clock. Mr Mansfield, she said, was very busy. Which was fine. Martha knew about being busy, and she couldn't afford to make a grand gesture and walk out in a huff. Lewis Mansfield was her best chance—OK, her only chance right now—of getting out to St Bonaventure, so she was just going to have to wait.

Only she wished that he would hurry up. Noah had woken up and was getting restless. Martha hoisted him out of his buggy and carried him over to look at the enlarged black and white photographs that lined the walls.

They were not very interesting. A road stretching out across a desert. A runway. A port. Another road, this one with a tunnel. A bridge. Dramatic in their own way, but personally Martha preferred a bit of life. Including a person in the shot would have given the structures some sense of scale and humanised the pictures. Now, if they had just had a model striding across the tarmac…

'I'm thinking like a fashion editor,' Martha told Noah. 'I'd better stop it, hadn't I? I've got a new career now.'

Could you call being a nanny for six months a career? It certainly wasn't the one she had had in mind when she left university. Martha thought about her exciting job at *Glitz*, and sighed inwardly. Somehow, being a nanny didn't have quite the same ring to it.

Noah, at eight months, was not yet up to much in the way of conversation, but he bumped his forehead affectionately against Martha's jaw in reply and she hugged him back. He was worth more than any dazzling career.

The door to Lewis Mansfield's office opened and Martha turned hopefully as his PA reappeared.

'Lewis will see you now,' she said. 'Sorry you've had to wait so long.' She looked a little doubtfully at Noah. 'Do you want to leave him with me?'

'Thanks, but now he's awake I think I'd better take him with me,' said Martha. 'Could I leave the buggy here, though?'

'Sure.' The PA lowered her voice and nodded her head towards the closed door. 'He's not in the best of moods,' she warned.

Oh, great, thought Martha, but it was too late to turn back now. 'Maybe he'll cheer up when he discovers that I'm the answer to his prayers?' she suggested, but the PA's answering smile was disturbingly sympathetic.

'Good luck,' was all she said.

Behind the closed door Lewis shuffled the papers morosely on his desk and waited for Martha Shaw to appear. To say that he was not in the best of moods was an understatement.

It had been a hellish day so far, kicked off bright and early by Savannah turning up on his doorstep in a terrible state, followed inevitably by reporters ringing the bell, eager to discover the sordid details of the last instalment in the long-running melodrama that was Savannah's relationship with Van Valerian.

He had finally calmed his sister down, fought his way through the pack of paparazzi at the door, and champed in frustration at endless traffic delays, only to get to work and discover one crisis after another, all of which had to be dealt with urgently. Just to make things more interesting, the nanny had turned up at lunchtime saying that her mother had been taken into hospital and dumping Viola with him until the evening.

At least Viola was behaving herself, thought Lewis. So far, anyway. He eyed the carry-cot in the corner dubiously. She was sleeping peacefully, but the way today was going that wouldn't last.

He would have to make the most of the time he had left today. He wished he hadn't agreed to see Martha Shaw, but Gill had been so insistent that her friend was just the person he needed to look after Viola that in the end he had given in just to shut her up. 'Martha will be absolutely perfect for you,' she had insisted.

Lewis wasn't so sure. Gill was a friend of Savannah's and worked on some glossy, glittery magazine. He couldn't imagine her being friends with a nanny at all, let alone the kind of calm, sensible, solid nanny that he wanted.

The door opened. 'Martha Shaw,' said his PA brightly, and ushered in exactly the kind of woman Lewis least wanted to see right then.

He should have known, he thought bitterly, taking in the slightly dishevelled glamour and the brittle smile. She was attractive enough, with a swing of dark straight hair and that generous mouth, but she was far too thin. Lewis preferred women who didn't look as if they would snap in two the moment you touched them.

So much for a calm, solid nanny. Martha Shaw radiated nervous exhaustion. Her huge dark eyes were smudged with tiredness, and she held herself tensely.

And she wasn't just holding herself.

'That,' said Lewis, ignoring her greeting and levelling an accusing stare at her hip, 'is a baby.'

Martha followed his gaze to Noah, who was sucking his thumb and gazing around him with round blue eyes. Nothing wrong with Lewis Mansfield's powers of observation then, even if his manners left something to be desired.

'Good heavens, so it is!' she exclaimed with an exaggerated start of surprise. 'How did that get there?'

Her facetiousness was met with a scowl that made her heart sink. Not only was Lewis sadly lacking on the courtesy front, but he clearly had no sense of humour either. *Not* a good start to her interview.

Time to try charm instead. 'This is Noah,' she said with her best smile.

It was not returned. Somehow she hadn't thought that it would be. Lewis Mansfield was the walking, talking embodiment of dour. He was tall and tough-looking, with an austere, angular face and guarded eyes. It was hard to believe that he could be related in any way to the golden, glamorous Savannah Mansfield, with her famously volatile temper and celebrity lifestyle.

Gill might have warned her, thought Martha with a touch of resentment. Admittedly, Gill had said that Lewis could be a bit gruff. 'But he's a sweetie really,' she had hastened to reassure Martha. 'I'm sure you'll get on very well.'

On the receiving end of his daunting glare, Martha somehow doubted that.

She studied Lewis with a dubious expression as she waited for him to apologise for keeping her waiting, or at least to ask her to sit down. Very dark, very thick brows were drawn together over his commanding nose in what looked suspiciously like a permanent frown, and she searched in vain for any sign of softness or sensitivity in the unfriendly eyes or that stern mouth. He looked grim and grumpy and, yes, definitely gruff, but a *sweetie*? Martha didn't think so.

'He's very good,' she offered, ruffling Noah's hair when it was obvious that no apology would be forthcoming.

They could hardly stand here all afternoon glaring at each other, so one of them was going to have to break the silence and it looked as if it was going to have to be her. She hoped Lewis couldn't see her crossed fingers when she thought about all the broken nights. 'He won't be any trouble.'

'Hah!' grunted Lewis, prowling out from behind his desk. 'I've heard *that* before—usually from women who promptly hand over their babies and go off, leaving you to discover for yourself just how *much* trouble they are!'

Oh dear, this wasn't going well at all. Martha sighed inwardly. Gill had given her the impression that Lewis Mansfield was a frazzled engineer, struggling to build up his own company and overwhelmed by the unforeseen responsibility of looking after his sister's baby. She hadn't actually *said* that he was tearing his hair out and desperate for help, but Martha had come fully expecting him to fall on her neck with gratitude for turning up just when he needed her.

Dream on, Martha told herself wryly. One look at Lewis Mansfield and it was obvious that he wasn't the demonstrative type. He didn't look the slightest bit desperate or overwhelmed, and as for feeling grateful...well, there clearly wasn't much point in holding her breath on *that* front!

She thought about St Bonaventure instead and forced a cheerful smile. 'That's why I'm here,' she pointed out, and sat down on one of the plush black leather sofas.

To hell with waiting to be asked, she thought. Noah was heavy and she was tired and her feet hurt. If Lewis Mansfield didn't have the common courtesy to ask her to sit down, she would sit anyway.

She settled Noah beside her, ignoring Lewis's look of alarm. What did he think Noah was going to do to his swish sofa? she wondered, exasperated. Suck it apart? He was only eight months. He didn't have the teeth or the hands for wholesale destruction.

Yet.

'Gill said that you're looking after your sister's baby for a few months,' she persevered. 'I gather you're going out to the Indian Ocean and will take the baby with you, so you need someone to help. Gill suggested I could be the someone who makes sure that she isn't any trouble to you while you're away.'

'It's true that I need a nanny,' said Lewis, as if unwilling to admit even that much. 'Savannah—my sister—is going through a very…stressful…time,' he said carefully, as if Martha wouldn't have read all about his sister's tempestuous affair, wedding and now divorce in the pages of *Hello!*

'She's finding it hard to cope with the baby and everything else that's going on at the moment,' he went on, 'and now she wants to check herself into a clinic to sort herself out.'

Martha knew about that too. *Hello!* was required reading in the *Glitz* offices and it was a hard habit to kick. She didn't blame Lewis Mansfield for the faint distaste in his tone. Savannah Mansfield was ravishingly pretty, but she had always struck Martha as a spoilt brat who was far too prone to tantrums when she didn't get her own way. Her marriage to the brooding rock star Van Valerian, not renowned for the sweetness of his own temper, had been doomed from the moment their engagement was announced with full photo coverage and much flaunting of grotesquely large diamond rings.

Now Savannah was checking herself into a clinic famous for its celebrity clientele, most of whom seemed to Martha to be struggling solely with the pressure of being too rich and too thin. Meanwhile poor little Viola Valerian had been abandoned by both parents and handed over to her grim uncle.

Martha felt sorry for her. Lewis Mansfield might be a responsible figure, but he didn't look as if he would be a very jolly or a very loving one.

Which was a shame. It wasn't that he was an unattractive man. Her dark eyes studied him critically. If he smiled he could probably look quite different, she thought, her gaze lingering on the stern mouth, but when she tried to imagine him smiling or loving a queer feeling prickled down her spine and she looked quickly away.

'Who's looking after Viola at the moment?' she asked, really just for something to say while she shook off that odd sensation.

'Her nanny. She's been with Viola since she was born, but she's getting married next year and she doesn't want to be away from her fiancé for six months.'

It seemed fair enough to Martha, but Lewis sounded impatient, as if Viola's poor nanny was being completely unreasonable in wanting to stay with the man she loved.

'I need someone experienced at caring for babies who's prepared to spend six months in St Bonaventure,' he went on, and Martha straightened her back, pleased that they had at last come to the point.

'I'm your gal!' she told him cheerfully. 'You need someone who knows how to deal with babies. I know how to deal with babies. You want someone who doesn't mind going to St Bonaventure for six months. I want to go there for six months. I'd have said we were made for each other, wouldn't you?'

She should have known better than to be flippant. Lewis regarded her with deep suspicion. 'You don't look much like a nanny to me,' he said finally.

'Well, nannies nowadays don't tend to be buxom and rosy-cheeked old retainers,' Martha pointed out.

'So I'm discovering,' said Lewis glumly. He was obviously hankering after a grey-haired old lady who had been with the family for generations and who would call him Master Lewis.

Come to think of it, why *didn't* the Mansfields have someone like that to call on? Martha wondered. She didn't know much about them, but they had always sounded a famously wealthy family, the kind that threw legendary parties and flirted with scandal and generally amused themselves without ever doing anything useful.

At least, that was how she had thought of them until she met Lewis. Perhaps he was a throwback?

'We may not be very good at tugging our forelocks, but it doesn't mean that modern nannies don't understand babies just as well,' she said, and smiled fondly down at Noah, who had propped himself up on one chubby hand and was patting the leather cushion with a puzzled expression. He hadn't come across anything quite so luxurious before.

'I suppose so.' Lewis sounded unconvinced, and was obviously eyeing Noah's exploration of his sofa askance.

Martha dug around in the capacious bag she always carried with her now and pulled out a rattle to distract Noah. Grabbing it, he shook it energetically and squealed with delight. The sound that it made never failed to amuse him, and the way his round little face split into a smile never failed to squeeze Martha's heart.

He was so adorable. How could anyone resist him?

Glancing back at Lewis, she saw that he was resisting Noah's appeal without any trouble at all. Still, at least he had come to sit on the sofa opposite her. That was something, Martha thought hopefully.

'Is this your current charge?' he asked, as if Noah were some kind of bill.

'He's my permanent charge,' Martha told him, pride

creeping into her voice. 'Noah is my son,' she added patiently when it was clear that Lewis was none the wiser.

'Your *son*?' He didn't actually recoil, but he might as well have done. 'Gill didn't mention anything about you having a baby.'

Gill hadn't mentioned anything about him being the human equivalent of the north face of the Eiger either, thought Martha. You could hardly hear yourself think for the sound of illusions being dashed all round.

Not that she really blamed Gill. The other woman had taken over from her as fashion editor at *Glitz*, and she was clearly keen to pack Martha off to the Indian Ocean where she wouldn't be in a position to angle for her old job back. Martha could have told Gill that she was welcome to the job, and she certainly would have done if it had meant that she had been rather better prepared to face Lewis Mansfield.

As it was, things seemed to be going from bad to worse. She would never get to St Bonaventure at this rate.

'I'm sorry,' she said carefully. 'I assumed that Gill would have told you about Noah.'

'She just said that you were experienced with babies, that you were free for six months and that you could leave almost immediately,' said Lewis, as if bedgrudging allowing even that much. 'She also said that you were very keen to go to St Bonaventure.'

Thanks, Gill, said Martha mentally, revising her earlier, less grateful opinion of her successor.

'All that is true,' she told Lewis. 'I'm very—'

She stopped as Noah threw his rattle at Lewis with a yell. 'Shh, darling,' she admonished him, reaching over to retrieve the rattle, but it was too late. The baby sleeping in the carrycot had woken up and was uttering sputtering little cries that signalled a momentous outburst.

Lewis rolled his eyes. 'That's all I need!'

Leaping to her feet before Lewis could get too harassed, Martha went over to pick up Viola and cuddled her against her shoulder until her cries subsided into hiccuping little sobs.

'Now, let's have a look at you,' she said, settling back on the sofa and turning Viola on her knee so that she could examine her. 'Oh, you're very gorgeous, aren't you?'

All babies were adorable as far as Martha was concerned, but Viola was exceptionally beautiful, with her golden curls, pansy-blue eyes and ridiculously long lashes where the tears still shimmered like dewdrops. She looked doubtfully back at Martha, who smiled at her.

'I think you probably know it too, don't you?' she said, and Viola dissolved into an enchanting smile that in anyone older than a baby would have undoubtedly been classified as a simper.

'How old is she?' Martha asked Lewis as she tickled Viola's tummy and made her giggle.

'What?' Lewis sounded distracted.

'She looks about the same age as Noah.'

Annoyed for some reason by the unexpected sweetness of Martha's smile, Lewis pulled himself together with an effort. How old *was* Viola?

'She's about eight months,' he said after a mental calculation.

'Oh, then she is the same as Noah.'

Noah was beginning to look a bit jealous of all the attention Viola was getting, so Martha put them both on the carpet where they could sit and subject each other to their unblinking baby stares. She watched them fondly for a moment.

'They could almost be twins, couldn't they?'

'Apart from the fact that one's blonde and the other is dark?' countered Lewis, determined not to be drawn into any whimsy.

'OK, not identical twins,' said Martha mildly. 'When's Viola's birthday?'

'Er...May ninth, I think.'

'Really?' Forgetting his disagreeable manners, Martha beamed at Lewis in delighted surprise. 'That's Noah's birthday, too! Isn't that a coincidence? You really are twins,' she told the two babies on the floor, who were still eyeing each other rather uncertainly.

She glanced back at Lewis. 'It must be fate,' she said hopefully.

Lewis looked discouraging, not entirely to Martha's surprise. She hadn't really expected him to be the type who set much store by signs and superstitions and intriguing coincidences. No point in bothering to ask him his star sign, she thought resignedly. He was the kind of man who would just look at you in disgust and not only not care what sign he was but not even know.

'You haven't told me why you're so keen to go to St Bonaventure,' he said, disgruntled in a way he couldn't even explain to himself. It was something to do with the way she had held Viola, with the way she had smiled at the two babies on the floor, with the way her face had lit with surprise. He didn't have time to notice things like that, Lewis reminded himself crossly.

'Does one need a reason to want to spend six months on a tropical island?' Martha turned his question back on him. Her voice was light, but Lewis had the feeling she was holding something back and he frowned.

'I'd want to feel that a nanny who came with us knew exactly what she was getting into,' he said repressively. 'St Bonaventure is isolated, in the middle of the Indian Ocean, and whichever direction you turn it's hundreds of miles to the nearest major city. The island is very small, and once you've been round it there's nowhere else to go except for a scattering of even smaller islands with even less to see.'

It was at that point that Viola, after subjecting Noah to a long, considering stare, reached out deliberately and pushed him over. Startled, Noah let out a wail, and Lewis looked irritated.

Oops, maybe putting the babies together wasn't such a good idea after all. Martha scooped them both up and settled them on either side of her, giving Noah his rattle and finding Viola a dog-eared toy which she promptly stuffed in her mouth.

'Sorry about that.' Martha looked back at Lewis. 'You were saying?' she asked him politely.

Lewis watched his niece glaring haughtily over Martha's lap at Noah and looking for a moment so like her mother that he almost laughed. He glanced at Martha with reluctant respect. He had to admit that she seemed surprisingly competent for such an unlikely-looking nanny.

Viola, as her current nanny was always telling him, could be a handful, and if she took after her mother, as she was already bidding fair to do, that would turn out to be a masterly understatement. But Martha seemed to have got her measure straight away, dealing with her with a combination of tenderness and firmness.

Belatedly, Lewis became aware that Martha had asked him a question and was waiting expectantly for the answer. Cross with himself for letting himself get diverted from the issue, he scowled.

'You were telling me about conditions on St Bonaventure,' Martha prompted kindly.

Not that that made Lewis feel any better. He didn't like looking foolish, and he suspected that was *exactly* how he did look right then. Abruptly getting to his feet to get away from that dark stare, he prowled around the room.

'The island was hit by a cyclone last year which wiped

out most of the infrastructure. That's why I'm going,' he told her. 'The World Bank is funding a new port and airport with access roads, so it will be a major project.'

'But surely all that will take longer than six months?' said Martha in surprise.

Lewis gave a mirthless laugh. 'It will certainly do that! We're going to be doing the design and overseeing the construction, so there'll be a resident engineer out there for the duration of the project, but I want to be there for the initial stages at least. It's a prestigious project and this is a critical time for the firm. We need it to be a success.'

'So you'll spend six months setting everything up and then come back to London?'

'That's the plan at the moment. I might end up staying longer—it depends how things go. We'll need to do various surveys, which may mean incorporating various changes into the design, and it's important to establish a good working relationship with all the authorities and suppliers. These things take time,' said Lewis, very aware of Martha's eyes on him.

He wished she would stop looking at him with that dark, disturbing gaze, stop sitting there with a baby tucked under either arm, stop being so...*unsettling*.

'In any case, Savannah should be able to look after Viola herself in six months' time,' he concluded brusquely, uncomfortably conscious that he had lost the thread of what he was saying. Martha didn't need to know about the project, or why it was important to him. Anyone would think he *cared* what she thought. 'It would be a strictly short-term contract as far as a nanny is concerned.'

'I understand,' said Martha.

'The point I'm trying to make is that it's not going to be an extended beach holiday,' Lewis persevered. 'St Bonaventure isn't developed as far as tourism goes, and there's a very small expatriate community. I'm going to be extremely busy, and will be out all day and probably a number of evenings too.

'Whoever comes out to look after Viola is going to be in for a very quiet few months. She's going to have to look after herself. Sure, the weather's nice, but once you've been down to the beach there's nowhere else to go and nothing else to do. The capital, Perpetua, is tiny and there are hardly any shops, and where you do find one it's dependent on imports that can be erratic, to say the least. Sometimes the shelves are empty for months, which can make the diet monotonous.'

'I think you've made your point,' said Martha, smiling slightly, as if she knew that he was doing his damnedest to put her off and wasn't having any of it.

Lewis scowled and dug his hands in his pockets. 'All I'm trying to say is that if you're expecting paradise you'd better think again!'

Martha met his gaze directly. 'I'm not looking for paradise in St Bonaventure,' she said.

'What are you looking for, then?'

For a moment, Martha hesitated. She had hoped that it wouldn't be necessary to tell Lewis Mansfield the whole story at this stage, but it was probably better to be open.

'I'm looking for Noah's father,' she said clearly.

If she had expected a sympathetic response from Lewis she was doomed to disappointment. 'Careless of you to lose someone as important as that,' he commented, and then lifted a sardonic eyebrow. 'Or did he lose you?'

Martha flushed slightly. 'It wasn't like that. Rory is a marine biologist. He's doing a PhD on something to do with ocean currents and coral reefs…I'm not sure exactly, but he's doing his fieldwork on some atoll off St Bonaventure.'

'If you know where he is, he's not exactly lost, is he? Why do you need to go all the way out to the Indian Ocean when you could just contact him? If he's a student he's bound to have an email address, if nothing else. It's not hard to track people down nowadays.'

'It's not that easy,' said Martha. 'I need to see him. Rory doesn't know about Noah, and it's not the kind of thing you can drop in a casual email. What would I say? *Oh, by the way, you're a father*?'

'It's what you're going to have to say when you see him, isn't it?' Lewis countered.

Martha bit her lip. 'I think it would be better if Rory could actually see Noah. He won't seem real to him otherwise.'

'You mean you think you're more likely to get money out of him if you turn up with a lovely, cuddly baby?'

The dark eyes flashed at his tone. 'It's not about money,' she said fiercely. 'Rory's a lot younger than me. He's still a student and finds it hard enough to survive on a grant himself, never mind support a baby. I know he can't afford to be financially responsible for Noah, and I'm not asking him to.'

'Then why go at all?'

'Because I think Rory has the right to know that he's a father.'

'Even though presumably he wasn't interested enough to keep in touch with you and find out for himself that you were all right?'

'It wasn't like that,' said Martha a little helplessly. How could she make someone like Lewis understand?

'I met Rory at the beginning of last year. It wasn't just a one-night stand,' she added, hating the idea that he might think there had been anything sordid or casual about the affair. 'I liked Rory a lot and we had a very nice time together but at the same time we both knew that it wasn't a long-term thing.

'We had completely different lives, for a start. He was

only in the UK to go to conferences and write up some of his research, and I had a great job in London. It was always clear that he had to go back to St Bonaventure to finish his thesis, and we both treated it as...' she shrugged lightly, searching for the right description '...as a pleasant interlude.'

'So he didn't know you were pregnant?'

'Yes. I found out just before he left, so I told him. I felt I had to.'

'And he left anyway?' Lewis sounded outraged and Martha looked at him curiously.

'We discussed it,' she told him, 'and we agreed that neither of us was ready to start a family. It was obviously out of the question for him, and I was very involved in my own career. I was incredibly busy then too. There was no way I could imagine fitting a baby into my life...'

She trailed off as she remembered how obvious everything had seemed at the time. 'Anyway,' she went on, recollecting herself, 'the upshot was that I told Rory that I was going to be sensible. I said he didn't need to worry, I would take care of everything.'

For a moment the image of Rory's expression of stunned relief as he realised what she was saying was vivid in her mind. 'It didn't feel like a big deal, then,' she remembered. 'I just thought it would be a straightforward operation and that I would be fine.'

Martha looked down at Noah and smoothed his dark, downy hair. Just the thought of how close she had come to never having him made her shudder now.

'So Rory went back to St Bonaventure,' she finished, glancing back at Lewis. 'And I...changed my mind.'

Of course she had changed her mind, thought Lewis with a jaundiced expression. Changing their minds was what women did, and to hell with the consequences for anyone else involved!

'Don't tell me,' he said dourly. 'Your body clock was ticking, everyone else was having babies and playing at being perfect mothers and you wanted to play too?'

Martha was taken aback by the edge of bitterness in his voice. What was his problem? Don't let him wind you up, she reminded yourself. He's your ticket to St Bonaventure.

'You might be right about the body clock,' she admitted honestly. 'I'm thirty-four, and with no sign of another serious relationship on the horizon I had to face the fact that might not have another chance to have a child. It hadn't been an issue before. I had a boyfriend for eight years and we were both thinking about our careers, not about babies. I thought I was fine with that, but once I was pregnant...it's hard to explain, but everything changed after Rory had gone. I just knew I couldn't go through with it and that I wanted to keep the baby.'

Lewis was looking profoundly unmoved by her story. 'Why didn't you tell him that you'd changed your mind?'

'I knew that he wasn't going to be in a position to help, and anyway I felt that it was my decision in any case. I didn't want Rory to feel responsible.'

'And now you've changed your mind about that too?'

Martha eyed him warily. There was a current of hostility in his voice that she didn't understand. She wasn't sure if it was women generally that he disliked or just single mothers, but there was certainly something about her that was rubbing him up the wrong way.

It was a pity, she thought. She had warmed to him while he was telling her about the project. Striding about the office, the austere face lit with enthusiasm, he had seemed warmer and more accessible somehow. More...well, attractive. She had even begun to think that spending six months with him wouldn't be so bad after all.

Now she wasn't so sure.

CHAPTER TWO

MARTHA set her chin. It didn't matter what Lewis Mansfield was like, or whether he liked her or not. The important thing was to convince him to give her the job. She needed to get out to St Bonaventure, and somehow he had to realise how important it was to her.

She glanced down at her small son. He was why she was here now. 'When Noah was born…' she began slowly, only to pause and rethink what she was trying to say. 'Well, it's hard to explain to someone who hasn't had a baby, but my life changed completely. It was as if everything had turned round and the things that had been important before suddenly didn't matter that much any more. The only thing that really mattered was Noah.

'I want to give him the things every child needs,' she went on, picking her words with care. 'Love, security, support…I can do all of that as a mother, but I can't be his father. The bigger Noah gets, the more I've come to realise that he needs a father as well as me. At the very least, he needs to know who his father is.'

She looked back at Lewis, her gaze very direct. 'I don't want Rory to feel that he has to provide any financial support, but I do want to give him the chance to be part of his son's life, even if it's only occasional contact.

'Of course I'm hoping that he'll want more than that, that he'll want to see Noah grow up and share his life as part of the family,' she said, 'but I'm not setting my heart on that because it might not be right for any of us. But I can't know any of that until I can find Rory himself and introduce him to Noah and that's why I need to get to St Bonaventure as soon as I can,' she finished breathlessly.

Lewis didn't respond immediately. Instead he came back to sit opposite her and regard her with an indecipherable expression.

'If it's so important to you, why don't you just buy a ticket, go out there and find this guy?' he asked at last. 'St Bonaventure is a tiny place. It's not going to be too hard to track him down. Why complicate matters by getting involved as a nanny?'

'Because I can't afford to get there any other way,' said Martha frankly. 'You said yourself that St Bonaventure is not a mass market destination for tourists. That means that there are no package deals, and all the flights I've looked into are phenomenally expensive, especially when I don't know how long it would take me to find Rory. I just don't have that kind of money at the moment.'

She had never met anyone who could use his eyebrows to the effect that Lewis did. One was lifting now, expressing disbelief and disdain in a way no words ever could. 'I'm no expert,' he said—and looking at his conventional suit and tie Martha could believe *that*!—'but those look like pretty expensive clothes to me.'

His slate-coloured gaze encompassed her soft suede trousers, the beautifully cut shirt and the stylish boots. There was nothing obvious about the way she dressed, but she still managed to ooze glamour. 'If you can afford to dress like that I'd have thought you could afford a plane ticket.'

'I bought this outfit a long time before I had Noah,' said Martha, acknowledging the point. 'I couldn't afford any of it now and, to be honest, I wouldn't buy it even if I could.' She looked ruefully down at the stains and creases that Lewis obviously couldn't see from where he was sitting. 'It's totally impracticable for looking after a baby!'

'Presumably when you talked about the great career you had, you didn't mean being a nanny then?' he asked sardonically.

'No. I was a fashion editor for *Glitz*. You won't know it,' she told him before he could say anything, 'but it's a glossy magazine for women, and very high profile. I loved my job and I had a good salary, but unfortunately I had a very expensive lifestyle as well.'

Martha sighed a little, remembering how carelessly she had bought shoes and clothes and the latest must-have accessories. The money she had spent on cabs alone would easily have kept her in St Bonaventure for a year.

'I used to eat out a lot, and had wonderful holidays…I suppose I wasn't very sensible,' she admitted, 'but I never thought about saving. It was just the kind of world where you live for the moment and let the future take care of itself.'

'Which is all very well until you get to the future.'

'Exactly,' she said ruefully.

'Couldn't you go back to work if money's that tight?'

'I tried after Noah was born, but it was just too difficult. I was so tired that I couldn't think straight for the first few weeks, and when I missed one meeting too many the editor said that she was sorry but she had to let me go. Which was a nice way of saying that she was sacking me.'

Martha shrugged slightly. 'I could see her point. I was wandering around like a zombie, and fashion shoots cost a lot of money. You can't afford to have models like the ones *Glitz* uses sitting around waiting for the fashion editor to remember what day of the week it is.'

'Perhaps you should have thought of that before you had a baby,' said Lewis astringently.

'I did think about it,' said Martha, keeping her voice even with an effort. 'That's why I didn't have a baby before, but I don't regret having Noah for a moment. I don't

want a demanding job that means I have to leave him all
day with someone else. I want to be with him while he's
small. I've done various bits of freelancing, but it's not
very reliable, and it doesn't help that I'd saddled myself
with a huge mortgage just before I met Rory.'

Martha winced just thinking about the money she owed
the bank. 'It's a fabulous flat—a loft conversion overlook-
ing the river—but I just can't afford to live in it now and,
anyway, it's totally unsuitable for a baby. I've got in ten-
ants and they're just covering the mortgage payments, so
Noah and I are living in a little studio, but frankly it's a
struggle even to pay the rent on that at the moment.'

'You could sell the flat that you own. If it's as smart as
you say it is, it ought to realise you some capital.' Lewis
was obviously of a practical turn of mind. Not that surprising in an engineer, now Martha came to think of it.

'I probably will,' she said, 'but I don't want to make
any decision until I've seen Rory. I can't really think about
what to do until I've done that. I just have the feeling that
once I know how he's going to react everything else will
fall into place, so getting to St Bonaventure is a priority
for me.'

She met Lewis's cool gaze steadily. 'That's why, when
Gill told me that you were going there and needed a nanny,
it seemed so perfect.'

'For you maybe,' he said with a cynical look. 'I'm not
sure what's in it for me if you're going to slope off in
search of marine biologists the moment you arrive.'

'There'd be no question of *sloping off*, as you call it.'
Martha took a deep breath and forced herself to stay calm.
'I assume that you would provide a proper contract for six
months, and I would certainly abide by it. That would give
me plenty of time to find Rory, introduce him to Noah and
get him used to the idea of having a son, and he wouldn't
feel rushed into making a decision. If at the end of that

time he wanted us to stay, fine. If not, we would just come back with you and Viola. At least I would have done everything I could to make contact between Noah and his father.'

Viola was getting bored. She started to squirm and Martha lifted her on to her knee, distracting her with another toy from her bag. Satisfied, Viola dropped the rabbit that she had been sucking and grabbed the rubber ring instead.

This left the rabbit free to be handed quickly to Noah, whose little mouth was turning ominously down as he watched his mother giving his rival all the attention. He accepted the rabbit, but very much with the air of one who was prepared to be diverted for now, but would be returning to the main point at issue before long.

Lewis watched Martha juggling the two babies and his brows drew together. 'It's just not practicable for you to be a nanny,' he said brusquely. 'You can't manage two at once.'

'Why not? Neither of them are crying, are they?' asked Martha, praying that Viola and Noah would stay quiet a little while longer.

'Not yet,' said Lewis. 'Jiggling them on your knee and giving them toys is all very well for five minutes, but what happens when both of them are screaming and need to be fed?'

'Mothers with twins manage.'

'Maybe they're used to it.'

'I'd get used to it too,' she said defiantly, but Lewis only scowled.

'Look at you,' he said, feeling cross and disgruntled without being sure why. It was something to do with the way she sat there and looked at him with those dark eyes. Something to do with the straightness of her back and the determined tilt of her chin.

'You look as if you haven't slept for a year,' he said roughly. 'I'm surprised you can cope with one baby, let alone think about looking after two.'

She looked as if she could do with six months in the sun, fattening herself up and catching up on sleep, he thought, and then caught himself. Martha Shaw wasn't his responsibility. It wasn't his fault she was tired. She had chosen to have a baby on her own, and it was too late to complain that it was tiring now.

Although she hadn't actually complained at all, had she? Lewis pushed the thought brusquely away. No, it was out of the question.

'I don't want to find myself looking after you and Noah as well as Viola,' he told her.

Martha wasn't ready to give up yet. 'I'm tougher than I look,' she said. 'I've been looking after a baby for the past eight months and I think I've probably got a better idea than you of what's involved,' she added, with just a squeeze of acid in her voice. 'I'm sure I would be able to cope.'

It went against the grain to plead with Lewis Mansfield, but if she had to she would. 'Please take me with you. I'd love Viola and look after her as if she really was Noah's twin.' She hesitated. How could she make him see how perfectly their needs matched? 'I think we're made for each other,' she said.

Wrong thing to say. One of Lewis's eyebrows shot up and, hearing her own words, Martha could have bitten her tongue out. And then she had to go and make matters worse by actually blushing!

'You know what I mean,' she muttered.

'I know what you mean,' Lewis agreed dryly as he got to his feet again. Really, the man was as restless as a cat. He took another turn around the room, his shoulders hunched in a way that was already oddly familiar.

'I should tell you that I only agreed to see you as a favour to Gill,' he said brusquely at last. 'Oddly enough, she was very insistent that you were just what I needed too.'

'I think I could be,' said Martha, determined not to repeat her mistake and forcing herself to sound suitably cool, as if the idea that they might be made for each other as lovers had never even crossed her mind.

Lewis wasn't so sure. He couldn't help thinking about what it would be like to share a house with her, to spend the next six months with those dark eyes and that mouth. It would be too distracting, too unsettling, too…too *everything*.

And she was totally unsuitable as a nanny anyway, he reminded himself. There was no way he was going to risk it.

'Perhaps I should have told Gill that I was seeing someone else as well,' he said, pushing away the thought of living with Martha for six months. 'The agency that supplied Viola's current nanny sent along someone this morning and I have to say that she seemed very suitable. Eve is a trained nanny, and she is obviously very…'

Dull was the word that leapt to mind. Lewis forced it down.

'…very efficient,' he said instead.

'Babies don't need efficiency,' said Martha before she could help herself. 'They need love and warmth and routine.'

'Eve comes with very good references so I'm sure she understands exactly what babies need,' said Lewis austerely. 'She's…'

Dull, insisted that wayward voice inside him.

'…a sensible girl…'

Dull.

'…and she doesn't have any other commitments…'

Dull.

'...so she can concentrate on Viola in a way that you wouldn't be able to,' he went on with an edge of desperation.

Yes, but she's dull.

'I need to bear in mind too that I'll be sharing a house with Viola's nanny for six months, so it's important to give the job to someone compatible. Eve seems a quiet, level-headed...'

Dull.

'...reliable person, and I'm sure she'll adapt to the routine out there very quickly.'

Yes, and she'll be very, very dull.

But she wouldn't have dark, disturbing eyes and she wouldn't put him on edge just by sitting there the way Martha did. It would be much better that way.

Dull, but better.

'I see.' Martha got to her feet and handed Lewis his niece, who glared at him.

I'm with you, Viola, thought Martha wryly.

'In that case, there doesn't seem much more to say.'

Determined not to let him see how desperately disappointed she was, she bent to retrieve the toys, stuffed them in her bag, and scooped up Noah. 'Thank you for taking the time to see me,' she said in a cool voice.

Lewis held Viola warily. He could feel her small body revving up to protest as Martha turned to go and she realised that she was going to be abandoned.

'I'm sorry,' he said abruptly, as if the words had been forced out of him against his will. 'I just don't think it would have worked out.'

Dispiritedly, Martha scraped up another spoonful of purée and offered it to Noah, who pressed his lips together and shook his head from side to side in a very determined manner.

Rather like Lewis Mansfield, in fact.

'Why,' asked Martha severely, 'are you men all being so difficult at the moment?'

Noah didn't reply, but he didn't open his mouth either. He could be very stubborn when he wanted.

Also like Lewis Mansfield.

With a sigh, Martha put the spoon in her own mouth and returned to her perusal of the small ads. She had reluctantly decided that she was going to have to put St Bonaventure on the back boiler for a while and find herself another job. The trouble with most part-time jobs was that they didn't pay enough to cover the costs of child care, but she was seriously considering going for a post as a housekeeper or a nanny, where she could take Noah with her and save herself the huge cost of renting even this tiny little flat.

Here was a job in Yorkshire...maybe she could apply for that?

Or maybe not, she decided, as she read to the end of the advertisement. That enticing heading should have read: 'Wanted, any idiot to be overworked and underpaid.'

Martha sucked the spoon glumly and was just turning the page when the phone rang. This would be Liz with her daily phone call to cheer her up.

'Hi,' she said, wedging the phone between her shoulder and her ear and not bothering to take the spoon out of her mouth.

'Is that Martha Shaw?'

Martha nearly choked on the spoon, and the phone slipped from her ear. She had no problem identifying that austere voice, although she was damned if she would give Lewis Mansfield the satisfaction of admitting it.

Hastily rescuing the phone before it fell on the floor, she removed the spoon and cleared her throat.

'Yes?' It came out a little croaky, but she didn't think she sounded too bad.

'This is Lewis Mansfield.'

'Yes?' That was much better. Positively cool.

'I was wondering if you were still interested in coming out to St Bonaventure to look after Viola,' he said, and Martha was delighted to hear the reluctance in his voice.

It was obvious that Lewis Mansfield would rather be doing anything than ringing her up, so something must have gone wrong with his oh-so-sensible plans. He must be desperate, in which case there would be no harm in making him grovel a little!

'I thought you already had the perfect candidate...what was her name again?'

'Eve,' said Lewis a little tightly.

'Ah, yes, Eve. Didn't she want the job?'

'She said she did, and I made all the arrangements, but she's just rung me to say that she doesn't want to go after all.'

'Oh dear,' said Martha, enjoying herself. 'That doesn't sound very reliable of her.'

'The point is,' said Lewis through gritted teeth, 'that we were booked to fly out this weekend and I haven't got the time to re-advertise. If you can be ready to leave then, I'll get a ticket for you and your baby.'

Martha settled back into her chair and took another spoonful of Noah's purée. 'But what about how incompatible you think we are?'

'I didn't say that.'

'You implied it.'

'Well, we'll both just have to make an effort.' Lewis was beginning to sound impatient. 'I've got a job to do, and I won't be around very much in any case.'

There was a tiny pause. 'You know, the right answer there was, "Don't be silly, Martha, I don't think we're incompatible at all, I think you're very nice",' said Martha tartly.

Lewis sighed. 'If you come to St Bonaventure we're just going to have to get on,' he said.

'You make it sound as if it's going to be a real chore!' Martha was obscurely hurt. 'What a pity I can be sensible and reliable and...what was it now?...oh, yes, *efficient*, like Eve!'

'The point about Eve was that she didn't have any other commitments,' said Lewis, exasperated. 'I hope that you *will* be sensible and reliable and efficient—and tougher than you look! You're going to need to be.'

'I'm all those things,' she said sniffily. Shame he hadn't given her the chance to prove it when he saw her!

'And, frankly, *I'm* desperate,' he said. 'I'm not going to grovel or pretend that it was you I wanted all along. I haven't got time to play games. You said you wanted to get out to St Bonaventure,' he went on crisply, 'and now I'm offering you the chance. If you take the job I'll courier round details and tickets to you tomorrow. If you don't want it, just say so and I'll make other arrangements.'

He would too. Martha wasn't prepared to risk it.

'I'll take it,' she said.

Martha sipped her champagne and tried not to be too aware of Lewis sitting at the other end of the row. They had been given the front row in the cabin so that the two babies could sleep in the special cots provided and the other passengers had understandably given them a wide berth, leaving Lewis and Martha with four seats between them.

By tacit consent they had sat at either end of the row, leaving a yawning gap between them. There had been no chance to have a conversation at Heathrow, with all the palaver of checking in double quantities of high chairs and buggies and car seats. Even with most of it in the hold they still had masses of stuff to carry on board and, as both babies were wide awake at the time, they had both been occupied with keeping them happy until it was time to board.

But now Noah and Viola were asleep, the plane was cruising high above the clouds, and there was a low murmur of voices around them as the passengers settled down with a drink and speculated about the meal to come. And Martha was very conscious of the silence pooling between her and Lewis.

She was beginning to feel a bit ridiculous, stuck at one end of the row. They couldn't have a conversation like this, and it was going to be a long flight.

Making up her mind, she shifted one seat along, although it involved so much balancing of her glass and flipping out and putting away of trays in the arm of the seat, not to mention shifting all the baby paraphernalia from one seat to another, that by the time she was halfway through Martha was already regretting her decision and she felt positively hot and bothered by the time she finally collapsed into the seat.

Lewis was looking at her curiously. 'What are you doing?'

'I just thought I should be sociable,' she said, pushing her hair crossly away from her face. 'We can hardly shout at each other all the way to Nairobi.'

'I thought you might appreciate the extra room if you wanted to sleep,' said Lewis, effectively taking the wind out of Martha's sails. She hadn't expected him to have a considerate motive for putting himself as far away from her as possible!

'We haven't even had our meal,' she pointed out. 'I don't want to sleep yet

Uncomfortably aware that she sounded defensive, if not downright sulky, she forced a smile. 'This just seems like a good opportunity to get to know each other. We're going to be spending six months together, after all. Besides, it sounds as if the flight from Nairobi is going to be in a much smaller plane than this, so we're probably going to have to sit right next to each other on that. We might as well get used to the idea of being in close proximity!'

'We're certainly not going to get any closer than that,' said Lewis grumpily.

My, he was a charmer, wasn't he? Martha sighed inwardly.

'Look, I'll move back if you feel I'm invading your personal space,' she said huffily, putting her glass down and making to unfasten her seat belt.

'For God's sake, stay where you are,' he said irritably, and then he sighed.

'I'm sorry,' he said in a different voice, pinching the bridge of his nose. 'I've been very…preoccupied recently. Things are hectic in the office, half our projects seem to be in crisis, the negotiations for the St Bonaventure port have stalled, nothing's getting done. And then there's all this business with Savannah…' He blew out his cheeks wearily.

Martha couldn't help but sympathise. She had read in the gossip columns about the tempestuous scenes his sister had been throwing, the latest of which had resulted in the police being called to her house. In the end, Lewis had taken her to the clinic himself, running the gauntlet of the reporters at the gates who'd banged on the car windows and shouted questions about the most intimate details of his sister's life.

No wonder he was tired.

'My temper's short at the best of times,' he admitted,

'and I know I've probably been taking it out on everyone else. My PA couldn't wait to get rid of me yesterday!'

His mouth twisted ironically and he glanced at Martha. 'You're right, we should probably get to know each other better. I should have made more of an effort earlier.'

'You've had a lot on your mind,' said Martha a little uncomfortably.

Damn, just when she had got used to him being grumpy and disagreeable he had to go and throw her off balance by suddenly acting human! How difficult of him.

'Do you think we could start again?' he asked, making things even worse.

What could she say? 'Of course,' said Martha and held out her hand across the empty seat between them. 'I'm Martha Shaw. How do you do?'

The corner of Lewis's mouth quirked. 'Nice to meet you, Martha Shaw,' he said gravely, and reached across to shake her hand.

Martha wished he hadn't done that. The fingers wrapped around hers were warm and comfortingly strong, and the press of his palm sent a disquieting shiver down her spine.

Pulling her hand away, she took a steadying gulp of her champagne. It was too sweet, and she hadn't really wanted it anyway. She had written enough articles about the de-hydrating effects of long haul flights and how the best thing to do was just to drink plenty of water, but when Lewis had tersely asked for a bottle of water himself something perverse in her had made her turn to the flight attendant on her side of the plane and accept a glass of free champagne with a brilliant smile.

It had been silly, and it felt even sillier now that Lewis was turning out to be so unexpectedly approachable. Really, he was being quite nice.

So there was no reason why she shouldn't be able to think of something to say, was there?

No reason other than the tingle of her palm. And the fact that, even though she was staring desperately at the tiny plane heading steadily south across the map of the world on the screen above the travel cots, all she could see was his mouth, with its corner turned up in amusement, and its hint of warmth and humour.

No reason at all, then.

'So, what…' Mortified by the squeakiness of her voice, Martha cleared her throat and started again. 'What happened to Eve?'

'Eve?'

'The nanny who fitted your job description so perfectly,' she reminded him. 'You know, the one who was so reliable and sensible and efficient and lacking in commitments?'

'Oh. Yes.' Lewis had forgotten about Eve for a minute there.

He felt a little light-headed for some reason, which wasn't like him. It definitely wasn't anything to do with Martha's smile, or the depth of her eyes, or the sooty sweep of those lashes against her cheek. Obviously not.

Lewis looked at the glass of water in his hand. He couldn't even blame the feeling on alcohol. Must be the cabin pressure, he decided.

'Apparently Eve fell in love,' he said.

Martha shifted round in her seat to stare at him in surprise. 'In love?'

'So she said.' There was a tinge of distaste in Lewis's voice. 'I interviewed her on Monday, she accepted the job on Tuesday, on Wednesday night she met some man in a club and she rang me on Thursday morning to say that she was going to spend the rest of her life with him so she didn't want to come to St Bonaventure after all, thank you very much.'

'*Really?*' Martha laughed. 'So she turned out to be not so sensible after all?'

'You could say that. Turning down a perfectly good job to invest everything in a man you've only known for a matter of hours...it's a ridiculous thing to do!'

'It won't seem like that if she fell in love with him.'

'How can she be in love with him?' demanded Lewis with a return to his old acerbic tone. 'She doesn't know anything about this man.'

A flight attendant was hovering, offering Martha more champagne, but she shook her head. She wasn't going to compound her mistake. 'Could I have some water?' she asked as she put her empty glass back on the tray. Now who was the sensible one? she thought wryly.

'Ah, so you're not a believer in love at first sight,' she said with an ironic look. 'Now, why does that not surprise me?'

'Are you?'

Martha thanked the flight attendant for her water before turning back to him. 'I used to be,' she told him.

He hadn't expected her to say that. 'What changed your mind?' he asked curiously.

'Falling in love at first sight and discovering that it didn't last,' she said with a sad little smile. Her eyes took on a faraway look as she remembered how it had been. 'When I met Paul it was like every cliché you ever heard. Our eyes met across a crowded room, and I knew—or thought I knew—that he was the only man for me. We were soul mates. I spent the rest of the night with him, and we moved in together a week later. At least we didn't go as far as getting married,' she joked.

Her description of how she had fallen madly in love coincided with a twinge that made Lewis shift a little irritably in his seat. Maybe it wasn't cabin pressure? Maybe he was coming down with something after all?

'So what happened?'

Martha sighed. 'Oh, the usual...day to day living, routine, stressful careers. It's hard to keep up the magic against all that. Paul and I did our best, but the enchantment wore off eventually and, when it did, there was nothing left,' she said sadly.

'We carried on for a while, but it wasn't the same. Splitting up was awful. Somehow the fact that we'd started with such high expectations made the squabbling even worse, and everything ended up feeling much more bitter than if we'd never had those dreams at all.'

For a moment her shoulders slumped as she relived the misery of those last horrible months with Paul, and then she straightened and made a determined effort to push the memories away. 'I decided then that I wasn't going to go through that again. A successful relationship needs to be based on more than infatuation.'

Lewis lifted an eyebrow. 'Meaning what?'

'Meaning that I think it's better to be pragmatic than romantic when it comes to sharing your life with someone. I'm looking for friendship and respect and a shared attitude to the practicalities of life now. They're going to lead to a happier and more lasting relationship than any amount of physical attraction—although that always helps, of course!'

'So is that what you had with Noah's father…what was his name again?…Rory?' Lewis was horrified to hear the faintest tinge of jealousy in his voice.

Fortunately, Martha didn't seem to have noticed. She was shaking her head.

'No.' She smiled ruefully. 'To be honest, I think it was more a case of lust at first sight! I met Rory at a party. It wasn't long after I'd broken up with Paul and my confidence had taken a knock. I was feeling my age too. Suddenly I seemed to be hurtling into middle age with nothing to look forward to.

'And then I saw Rory,' she said, remembering. 'He's

quite a bit younger than me and incredibly good-looking. We were all pale and pasty after a London winter and he'd just breezed in from the Indian Ocean, all blond and tanned and gorgeous! When he walked into that party I swear every woman in the room sucked in her breath and her stomach! Rory could have had his pick. There were lots of really pretty girls there, even a few models, but he spent the entire evening with me. I suppose I was flattered.'

Lewis heard the undercurrent of secret amazement and pleasure she had felt that night in her voice, and wondered if she really didn't know how attractive she was. Personally, he wasn't surprised that Rory had singled her out. The intelligence and character in her face more than compensated for the fine lines round her eyes, and that lush mouth was much more tantalising than the perfect body or smooth, untried expression of a twenty-year-old.

'Rory was just what I needed after Paul,' Martha was saying. 'He made me feel desirable again. It wasn't love at first sight, no, but we did get on really well in spite of the difference in our ages. If we'd had longer together, who knows? Maybe we could have built a good long-term relationship but, as it was, he had to go back to St Bonaventure. We both knew that it was never going to be a permanent thing, so we just enjoyed it for what it was— a lot of fun.'

Lewis was getting a bit tired of hearing about Rory, who was so attractive and such fun and no doubt a real stud in bed, too, he thought sourly. 'Did the fun include getting pregnant?' he asked disapprovingly.

'No, that was an accident,' said Martha. 'We'd been to Paris for the weekend—Rory had never been and I used to go to all the fashion shows—so we thought we'd treat ourselves to a great meal on our last night, and I had oysters. *Big* mistake! I was on the pill, but those oysters definitely disagreed with me. I had an upset stomach for a couple of days after we got back and…well, it happens.'

She shrugged. 'A touch of food poisoning isn't the best of reasons to start a family, I know, but I wouldn't change Noah for the world now. Anyway,' she went on with a sideways glance at Lewis, 'you don't need to worry that I'll do an Eve and throw out all your arrangements by deciding I have met the man of my dreams on St Bonaventure. I'm too much of a realist about love now for that, and even if I wasn't quite frankly I'm too tired to fall in love at the moment!'

CHAPTER THREE

LEWIS'S hard gaze encompassed her pale face and the circles under her eyes. 'You look it,' he said roughly.

'Well, I certainly wouldn't recommend being a single mother to anyone who relies on her sleep,' said Martha with a wry smile.

'You must have known it would be hard work.'

She nodded. 'Yes, I did, but it's like everyone always says…you can say that you know looking after a baby will be tiring, but until you're actually doing it you have no conception of what sleep deprivation does to you or of just what ''tired'' can mean!'

Lewis hunched a shoulder. 'If it's that bad why do women go on and on about how they want to have babies?'

'Because the joy you get from your child is worth every sleepless night,' said Martha, leaning forward to stroke Noah's cheek. 'It's worth every day you get through like a zombie, every hour you spend worrying about whether he's healthy or happy or how you're going to afford to give him everything he needs.'

Lewis's mouth turned down at the corners. 'That sounds all very fine, but in my experience it's a lot more basic than that. I think a lot of women have children to fulfil their own needs. They think about how much they want to be loved or valued, not about how the child will feel.

'Half the time they have a baby just because it's fashionable,' he said contemptuously. 'A baby is the latest designer accessory. You can dress it up in rinky-dinky little outfits and show it off, which is fine until the fashion

41

changes and you've got to keep up, and then it's Oh, dear, now what am I going to do with the baby?'

'Give it to my brother to look after?' suggested Martha, unsurprised at the bitterness in his voice if that was what had happened with Savannah.

'Or a nanny or a mother-in-law or anyone else you can find to deal with all that messy, boring stuff as long as it doesn't stop you doing whatever you want to do!'

There was a little silence. Martha had the feeling that she was treading on dangerous ground. 'Why did you agree to look after Viola if you feel that way?' she asked cautiously after a moment.

'What could I do?' Lewis replied, hunching a shoulder. 'I had my sister in hysterics, the baby crying...'

He shuddered, remembering the scene. 'Savannah's out of control at the moment. She's behaving very badly, but she's still in no state to look after a baby properly. Viola's father is in the States at the moment—or he was last time I heard. Half the time he's too out of it to remember that he's got a daughter, let alone to look after her, and Viola certainly can't look after herself.' He sighed. 'I'm the only one who can be responsible for her at the moment. She's just a baby. I couldn't just say that she wasn't my problem.'

Martha studied his profile, oddly moved by his matter-of-fact attitude. He seemed so hard when you first met him, she thought, remembering how off-putting she had found that austere, unsmiling face and the uncompromising air of toughness and self-sufficiency, but underneath it all he was obviously a kind man, and a decent one.

Kindness and decency weren't qualities she had valued much when she was caught up in the frenetic whirl of activity at work and a hectic social life, but it didn't take long to learn how important they were when life became more difficult.

Knowing that Lewis had them made him seem a much nicer man.

And a much more attractive one.

The thought slid unbidden into Martha's mind and she jerked her eyes away from his face.

Don't even *think* about it, she told herself. It's one thing to realise that Lewis might not be quite as unpleasant as you thought, quite another to start thinking of him as attractive. He's your employer and you're going out to find Rory. Don't complicate the issue.

She took a sip of her water. Maybe she should have stuck to the champagne after all.

'You must be very close to your sister if you're the one she turns to for help,' she said after a while.

Lewis grimaced. 'It's partly my own fault Savannah is the way she is,' he said. 'Her mother left when she was only four, so she never had an example of good parenting. Michaela—her mother—was an heiress. She was very pretty and very spoilt, just like Savannah. After she divorced my father she went off to the States, but she was killed in a road accident a couple of years later. All her money was put in a trust fund for when Savannah was eighteen, and Savannah has been running through her inheritance ever since.'

'I didn't realise that she was your half-sister,' said Martha, wriggling round in her seat so that it was easier to talk.

'She's fourteen years younger than me, so I wasn't around all that much after I went to university. Poor kid, she didn't have much of a childhood, looked after by a succession of nannies and then packed off to boarding school. My father was never much of a hands-on parent at the best of times,' he added dryly, 'and once his business started going downhill he withdrew into himself even more. I think he forgot about Savannah's existence most of the time.

'I tried to do what I could for Savannah in the holidays, and when our father died she made her base with me, but she was sixteen by then and had got in with a crowd of wild friends.' Lewis sighed. 'I was always bailing her out of trouble. I blame myself sometimes. Maybe if I'd been firmer with her she'd be less spoilt now.'

'It wasn't your fault,' said Martha stoutly. 'It's hard enough for perfect, supportive parents to deal with ordinary adolescents, let alone troubled ones. You can only have been a young man. I don't see how you could have possibly done more than you did.'

Lewis looked a little taken aback by her support. 'Helen was always telling me I should be stricter with Savannah.'

A few tiny bristles went up on the back of Martha's neck. 'Helen?' she asked in a carefully casual voice.

'My girlfriend.'

Girlfriend? Martha was alarmed by the sinking feeling in her stomach. Why should she be so disappointed…? No, no, scrub *disappointed*, she told herself. That wasn't the right word at all.

Surprised, that was better. Why should she be so *surprised* that Lewis had a girlfriend? She guessed he was in his late thirties. He was intelligent, competent, solvent, and even not bad-looking—if you liked the dour, steely type, that was. Apparently straight, and nothing obviously kinky about him. Of *course* he had a girlfriend.

'We were together for years,' Lewis was saying, 'but she used to get very fed up when Savannah turned up drunk when we had friends round, or rang me in the middle of the night.'

Past tense. Phew! Martha relaxed, only to remember that if she hadn't been disappointed there was no reason to feel relieved, was there?

Unaware of Martha's convoluted mental exertions, Lewis was brooding about his sister. 'I'm sure Helen's right,' he said. 'I probably do encourage Savannah to depend on me too much, but in spite of all that money she hasn't had an easy time of things. Yes, she's been spoilt, but she's very insecure and I can't just turn her away when she needs help, can I? She can behave appallingly sometimes, but when it comes down to it she's still my little sister—'

He broke off suddenly. 'Why are you looking at me like that?' he demanded.

'I'm just thinking that it's a shame that you don't have any children,' said Martha, appalled to find herself blushing slightly. She hadn't meant to stare at him like that. 'Not many men have such a strong sense of family. Don't you want a family of your own?'

'No,' he said, his face hardening. 'Savannah's been quite enough family to deal with, thank you.'

'It would be different if you had your own children.'

He shook his head. 'I wouldn't risk it. There's too much grief when things go wrong.'

'And so much happiness when they go right,' countered Martha.

'You said yourself that having a baby is hard work and you spend most of your time exhausted.'

'Yes, but I also said that it was worth it. And I've been trying to manage on my own. It wouldn't be like that for you.'

'That's what Helen used to say. "It won't be like that for us."' Lewis shook his head. 'I didn't see why it should be different for us.'

'You're...um...not together any more, then?' asked Martha.

'No.' He glanced at her and then away. 'Helen and I

had what I thought was an ideal relationship. She's a beautiful, smart, very talented lady.'

Oh, good, thought Martha. The ex from hell.

Although what was it to her, after all? Martha scowled down into her glass of water. Water! What was wrong with her? She had been the ultimate party girl once, the queen of champagne sippers.

'We were together a long time,' Lewis was saying. 'I travel a lot, and she was busy training as a barrister.'

Excellent, a barrister! So Helen was not just beautiful and smart but a serious person. Not the kind of woman who stood around sipping champagne, then.

Oblivious to Martha's mental running commentary, Lewis was still telling her about his relationship. 'We both had our own lives, but we enjoyed the time we spent together and everything was perfect until one day she woke up with her hormones in overdrive.'

His mouth turned down at the edges, remembering. 'That's when she started lobbying for a baby. It wasn't about getting married for Helen. She just wanted a child. "This is the right time," she kept saying.'

'Well, maybe it was for her,' said Martha, beginning to feel a twinge of sympathy for Helen. She might have been intimidatingly clever and beautiful, but she obviously hadn't got very far with Lewis.

'It wasn't the right time for her career,' he said astringently. 'She'd worked incredibly hard and had just qualified. She should have been thinking about getting experience, not babies. I couldn't believe that she would even consider chucking it all in.'

Martha thought about her own career, not quite as impressive as Helen's perhaps, but still, it had meant a lot to her. 'It's surprising what women will give up for a baby.'

'Oh, she wasn't going to give up her career,' said Lewis with an edge. 'Oh, no. She was going to have the baby and then go back to work. I didn't see the point in bringing a child into the world just to hand it over to a nanny while Helen made a name for herself at the Bar. Helen told me I was the one being selfish,' he added ironically.

'What happened?'

'She gave me an ultimatum. Try for a baby, or she'd leave me.'

'And?'

'She left.'

'I'm sorry,' said Martha uncomfortably. She bit her lip. 'Do you ever think you made the wrong decision?'

'No,' said Lewis. 'I miss Helen sometimes. Quite a lot, to tell you the truth,' he admitted, swirling his water around in his glass. 'She's a really special person. Strong, ferociously intelligent, interesting…and very beautiful.' He glanced at Martha. 'Yes, I miss her, but I would have missed her anyway if she'd had a baby. She became so obsessive about it that everything changed in any case. God knows what it would have been like if we'd actually had a baby!'

'You might have felt differently if you'd had a child of your own,' Martha suggested.

'And if I hadn't?' he countered. 'It would have been too late then, wouldn't it?'

Martha had dreamed about landing in St Bonaventure. She had been thinking about getting there for so many months now that she was sure that when the moment actually came the scene would unroll exactly as she had imagined it.

The plane would drop slowly down over the ocean, whose deep blue would fade into turquoise lagoons. She would look down out of her window and see tiny boats out beyond the reefs, startling white beaches fringed with palm trees and everywhere the glitter of sun on the water, and the strain of the last few months would evaporate in the dazzling light. She would hold Noah in her lap and think about Rory and wonder whether by the time she left they would be a family.

Only it wasn't *quite* like that.

Forty minutes before they were due to land, great, dark rain clouds began boiling up around the plane, and it grew darker and darker. Rain streamed against the windows and the turbulence woke both babies, who screamed as the change in pressure hurt their ears.

Martha held Noah and tried to calm him, but Lewis seemed to be doing a much better job with Viola. He looked like a rock sitting there, as if he hadn't even noticed the terrifying way the wind was buffeting the plane around, his great hands holding the baby firmly against him as she snuffled into his shoulder, evidently soothed by the steady beat of his heart.

Lucky Viola, Martha thought involuntarily. She knew that Noah was picking up on her own fear and that was just making him worse, but how could she be calm when the plane was lurching up and down and the fuselage was shuddering and the only thing between them and the ocean was thirty thousand feet of precisely nothing?

Lewis glanced across at her. 'OK?'

'Oh, yes. Fabulous.' Martha caught her breath as the plane dropped into another air pocket and she bit her lip so hard it began to bleed. 'There's nothing like a bit of dicing with death before breakfast, is there?' she said, wiping the blood away and running her tongue over her bottom lip, but her voice was humiliatingly wobbly.

Lewis shifted Viola on to his other shoulder, holding her in place with one hand, and somehow managed to undo his seat belt and shift into the seat next to Martha's without being thrown off balance.

Quite calmly, he refastened the seat belt and settled Viola securely. 'Give me your hand,' he said.

Martha was cuddling a wailing Noah on her lap. She probably *could* spare a hand. It was embarrassing to admit how much she wanted to hold on to Lewis. Only because she was scared, of course.

If she was less scared, Noah might calm down. So it would probably be best for him if she did take Lewis's hand, wouldn't it?

Shifting Noah into the crook of her arm, she stuck out her free hand almost rudely. Lewis folded his fingers around it and rested their clasped hand on the armrest between them.

'You're quite safe,' he said. 'It's often like this in the rainy season. The pilots are used to it. In a little while we'll be dropping down below the clouds and it'll be much quieter.'

'Doesn't that depend on just how fast we'll be dropping?' said Martha edgily, trying not to notice how warm and comforting his hand felt. 'There's dropping and there's falling!'

The corner of Lewis's mouth twitched. 'We'll be making a controlled descent,' he said gravely. 'Does that make you feel better?'

Actually, what was making her feel better was the warmth of his fingers and the calmness of his voice. There was something incredibly reassuring about the way he sat there so relaxed and at ease, in spite of the baby clutching at his shoulder and the hysterical woman clutching his hand.

Martha's heartbeat slowed steadily and, sensing her growing confidence, Noah buried his face in her breast, his wails subsiding to woebegone sobs as he burrowed instinctively into her for comfort.

Martha hugged him close with one arm, thinking how comforting it would be if she could do the same to Lewis. You would really feel safe with that hard body shielding you, and his arm tight around you and…and good God! What was she *thinking*? Martha caught herself up guiltily.

Pull yourself together, woman, she told herself sternly. It's only a bit of turbulence. No need to lose your head completely.

She didn't let go of his hand, though.

'I wish I could cry like a baby sometimes,' she said shakily, by now more perturbed by her own wayward thoughts than the turbulence.

'I know what you mean.'

'You do?' Martha stole a glance at him under her lashes. He wasn't handsome, with that beaky nose and those intimidating brows, but there was a cool competence and a self-sufficiency about him that was appealing all the same. Looking at the firm jaw and the stern mouth, she couldn't imagine him ever crying.

'Babies have a nice life,' he explained. 'You sleep when you want, eat when you want, and you can let people know exactly what you're feeling. You just let it all out. When you're a baby you don't have to pretend to be happy when you're not, or brave when you're really scared,' he said, sliding a half-smile at Martha. 'You don't have to pretend that you like someone when you don't.'

Or that you don't like them when really you do. Martha half opened her mouth to say it, but then closed it again, afraid that Lewis might ask her what she meant.

Later, Martha couldn't remember what Lewis talked about during the long descent to St Bonaventure. She just kept clinging to his hand and let his calm, steady voice flow over her until at last the plane touched down. It was pouring, and the rain was still streaming against the cabin windows, but at least they were on the ground. That was all Martha cared about right then.

Except that there was no longer any reason to hold his hand.

'All right?' asked Lewis, loosening his clasp.

'Yes.' Reluctantly Martha disengaged her fingers. 'Thank you,' she muttered, and put both her arms around Noah to stop her hand sneaking back towards Lewis's. 'I'm not usually that pathetic.'

'Think nothing of it,' he said, putting a protesting Viola back in her cot while he picked up assorted baby equipment beneath their feet. 'It can be frightening the first time you go through turbulence like that.'

The babies were restless and grizzly as they waited in a rudimentary terminal for the bags and assorted baby equipment to be unloaded from the plane. Martha sat numbly on a plastic chair. She felt as if she had been travelling her entire life. She had no idea what time it was in St Bonaventure, or at home, or anywhere else. Her whole body was buzzing with exhaustion, and it was a huge effort to keep her eyes open.

Afraid that she would simply fall asleep if she sat there any longer, Martha got up and walked Viola up and down.

'I can see why they need a new airport,' she said to Lewis, who was eyeing the building assessingly. She hoped he wasn't planning on rebuilding it there and then. 'If our stuff doesn't arrive soon I think I'm going to keel over right here.'

When they made it through customs at last they were met by a smiling man who introduced himself as Elvis.

So this was where he came, thought Martha fuzzily.

'I'm your driver,' he said, beaming. 'Welcome to St Bonaventure.'

Martha looked outside. She had never seen anything like the rain that sleeted down, bouncing off the tarmac and swirling along the deep gutters. So much for paradise.

'Thank you.' She sighed.

The downpour made it hard to see much as Elvis drove them into town. Martha had a confused impression of ramshackle buildings, but it was hard to take in much when Viola, who was thoroughly bored with travelling by now, decided to express her displeasure by throwing a tantrum.

'You know, you're not the only one who's fed up,' Martha told her, as Viola squirmed and screamed and arched her little body in fury. Suddenly Lewis's decision to stay childless seemed much more understandable.

From the front seat, Lewis turned round and frowned at the noise, which was loud enough even to drown out the thunderous drumming of the rain on the car roof. 'Can't you do anything to quieten her down?' he asked, shouting to make himself heard.

Martha's head was aching. She felt like a zombie and all she wanted to do was sleep for a month. 'Well, I could throw her out of the window,' she snapped, 'but I didn't think that was really an option.'

Oh, God, now Noah was starting as well! Martha joggled him on her knee as best she could. 'Are we nearly there?' she asked Elvis in desperation.

'Two minutes,' he promised.

It was possibly the longest two minutes of Martha's life, but at last they drew up outside a wooden house set in a jungly garden. It had a wide verandah running all the way round it and a corrugated iron roof on to which the rain crashed, but that was all Martha had time to notice as they ran for cover. Even the few seconds it took to get from the car to the verandah was enough to leave them drenched.

Gasping, wiping the rain from her face, Martha found herself being introduced to a plump, motherly-looking woman not much older than she was.

'This is Eloise,' said Lewis. 'I've arranged for her to come in during the day and do the cooking and the housework, so all you have to do is look after the children.'

All? Martha shifted the still yelling Viola to her other

arm and jiggled Noah's buggy as he set up a wail as well. Life out here was going to be a doddle, then.

But she smiled at Eloise, who held out her arms for Viola. 'Let me say hello,' she said comfortably. 'I like babies.'

Viola looked extremely dubious, but submitted to being transferred and even stopped crying as she stared at the new face smiling at her. Martha flexed her aching arms and stooped to reassure Noah.

'Thanks,' she said gratefully. If Eloise was good with babies it would make things a whole lot easier.

Inside, the house was spacious and simply furnished. It was probably lovely and cool if you wanted to escape from the heat, but right then it seemed to Martha damp, dark and oppressive.

'Does it always rain like this?' she asked Eloise.

Eloise grinned and shook her head. 'Tomorrow it will be sunny,' she promised.

Martha couldn't imagine it.

By the time they had explored the house, set up the travel cots and unpacked the rest of the babies' stuff it was nearly six, according to Martha's watch, which she had set to local time, and the gloom had intensified into dark. Eloise said she was going home.

'I've left you some supper,' she said. 'You just need to heat it up.' Her face split into a wide smile. 'Have a good evening.'

'Evening?' Martha rubbed the back of her neck wearily as she watched Eloise put up a huge umbrella and disappear down the back steps. 'Do you think that means we'll be able to go to bed soon?'

'Not unless we can persuade these two that it's time to sleep first,' said Lewis, nodding to where Viola and Noah were sitting on a rug energetically thumping the floor with an assortment of toys scattered around them. 'They look suspiciously bright-eyed to me.'

Martha followed his gaze. It was true. After whinging most of the afternoon the two babies had suddenly taken on a new lease of life and looked wide awake.

'I'll give them a bath,' she said. 'With any luck that will make them think that it's bedtime.'

Lewis was unpacking papers from his briefcase. 'Do you need a hand?'

She hesitated. The obvious answer was 'no'. She was the nanny, and she had insisted that she could manage both children by herself.

Which she could do, Martha reminded herself. Once they got into a routine.

'It would make things quicker tonight,' she admitted, swallowing her pride.

Lewis dropped the last sheaf of papers on to the table. 'OK,' he said briskly. 'Let's do it.'

He sat on a stool in the tiled bathroom and watched as Martha put the babies in the bath. She was kneeling on the floor, the sleeves of her pale yellow shirt rolled up and her dark hair pushed behind her ears. Her eyes were huge in her pale face and her skin had the taut look of exhaustion, but there was no trace of impatience in her manner as she gently washed first one baby then the other. They were both sitting up, gurgling and squealing as they beat at the water with dimpled hands, clearly not exhausted at all.

It was all right for them, Lewis thought sourly. They had been able to sleep most of the way, while he and Martha had had to endure the long flight to Nairobi, an interminable delay there while they waited for their transfer, and then the cramped conditions of the little plane that had flown them the last leg.

Had Martha found it as uncomfortable as he had? She hadn't complained, but then perhaps she hadn't been bothered by the way their knees had kept touching, or by the constant brush of their arms.

She had been sitting so close that Lewis had been able to smell the fragrance that she wore. It wasn't one that he recognised. Helen's perfume had been more intense. Martha wore a light, refreshing scent that made him think of fresh herbs and long grass, with just a hint of spice, and it bothered him that once he had started noticing it he couldn't get it out of his mind.

And then they had run into those rain clouds. Lewis could still feel Martha's fingers digging into his hand. It had been just as well, really. The sharpness of her nails had kept him focused and distracted him from her warmth and her softness and the sheen of her hair.

'Hey!' As a particularly vigorous splash caught Martha in the eye she sat back on her heels, laughing, and glanced up at him. 'I'm glad some people are enjoying themselves anyway!'

Her brown eyes were alight with laughter and the warmth of her smile banished the tiredness from her face. She looked so different from the brittle woman who had walked into his office and, unprepared, Lewis was conscious of an unfamiliar feeling that stirred disquietingly inside him.

'Is something wrong?' she asked, puzzled by his arrested expression.

'No.' Lewis looked away. 'When do I get to do my bit?'

'Now.' Martha gave him a towel to spread on his knee and lifted Viola out of the bath. 'Can you dry her?'

She laid Noah on a towel on the floor and wrapped it round him so that she could dry him carefully. Lewis did the same for Viola, but his attention kept wandering away to where Martha was dusting her baby with powder, playing with his kicking feet and blowing kisses against his tummy so that he squealed with delight and clutched at her hair.

Lewis thought about that silky hair drifting over *his* stomach and swallowed hard. Damn. The last thing he needed was to start thinking about that kind of thing. He was Martha's employer, and she had agreed to live with him in the expectation that he would treat her with the respect he accorded any other employee.

Why had that stupid girl...what was her name again? Eve, that was it...why had she taken the ridiculous notion that she was in love into her head? She would have been a perfect nanny. She could have been here now and he wouldn't have been sitting here thinking about Martha's hair brushing his skin or feeling jealous of a *baby*, for God's sake!

If Eve hadn't fallen in love he wouldn't even have known that watching someone bath a baby could be such a turn-on. She would have been able to look after Viola on her own and he could have been going through the contract, the way he should be doing now, not sitting here in the bathroom with a baby on his knee.

'Here.' Martha tossed him the powder. 'Play with her a little. She needs a bit of attention.'

Lewis looked down at his niece's solemn face. It seemed to him that Viola had been demanding and getting attention for the past few hours, but if he concentrated on her he might forget about the way Martha was smiling and swinging her hair against a chuckling Noah and lifting him up and covering him with kisses...

Viola. Focus. Experimentally, Lewis tickled her bare tummy with a finger and was gratified to see her break into a beaming smile. He tried it again and she giggled and grabbed at his hand, so he smiled at her and she laughed back.

Maybe this baby business wasn't so difficult after all,

he thought, and then made the mistake of glancing up to find Martha watching him with amusement.

'She likes you,' she said. 'You should play with her more often.'

Feeling like a fool for some reason, Lewis tugged his finger out of Viola's clutches. 'The point of paying a nanny was that I didn't have to do any of this hands-on business,' he said brusquely to cover his embarrassment.

'Stop grumbling,' said Martha, refusing to be cowed by his glare. She was getting used to it now, anyway, and suspected it was more of a defence mechanism than a sign of anger. She reached for a clean nappy and deftly fastened it around Noah before snapping him into a Babygro.

'Viola's your own flesh and blood, for heaven's sake,' she went on, 'and I'm only asking you to dry her. Here, let me have her.'

Shuffling across on her knees, she scooped Viola up from Lewis's lap. 'You don't need to panic, I'll deal with her nappy. Could you hold Noah while I'm doing that, or would that be too much to ask?'

'Oh, all right,' said Lewis grouchily, and found a clean, plump, sweet-smelling baby deposited in his lap.

He and Noah eyed each other, and Lewis was convinced he could identify a smug look on the baby's face, as if he knew quite well what the strange man with the big hands had been thinking about his mother. When Noah reached out and twisted his nose, he was sure of it.

'Ouch!' he exclaimed involuntarily as Noah burst into giggles and reached out again to see if he could get the same reaction, but Lewis was ready for him this time and drew his head sharply out of range.

Martha laughed at his expression. 'It's surprising how strong those little fingers are, isn't it?'

'They certainly are.' Lewis rubbed his nose ruefully. 'I think I'll do the nappy next time!'

'I'll remember that when Viola's nappy gets a bit whiffy,' said Martha, hoisting the baby into her arms for a cuddle. 'Come on, you two, it's time for bed.'

CHAPTER FOUR

'It's funny, but I don't feel so tired any more,' said Martha, when they had given the babies a bottle and settled them for sleep. She closed the door gently on them and sent up a silent prayer that they would both fall asleep without any fuss.

'A few hours ago I was ready to sleep standing up, but I've woken up again now,' she told Lewis, who averted his eyes as she stretched.

'Do you want something to eat?' he asked gruffly. 'Eloise said she'd left something for us.'

Deciding she might be hungry after all, Martha followed him into the kitchen to inspect what was on offer. It didn't look very inspiring. Some cold rice, a brown, sloppy stew with unidentifiable ingredients, and a bowl of red sauce.

She and Lewis looked at it and then at each other.

'Maybe it will look more appetising when it's heated up,' Martha suggested hopefully.

It didn't, but they carried it through to the dining area anyway and sat down at the table. Martha helped herself to some rice and a little of the stew, and picked up her fork. 'Well…here goes.'

For a couple of minutes they ate in silence, but their forks moved more and more slowly until she looked up and met Lewis's eyes.

'This is…' she said indistinctly, chewing valiantly.

'…absolutely disgusting?' he suggested, and she put down her fork in relief.

'Revolting,' she agreed.

Lewis poked at the stew on his plate. 'What's that slimy stuff?'

'Okra, I think. I can't even guess at what the rest of it is.' She reached for the red sauce. 'Perhaps this'll cheer it up a bit.'

'Be careful,' said Lewis. 'It's probably quite hot.'

What did he think she was going to do? Empty the whole lot on to her plate? 'I'm not an idiot,' she said irritably, and took a tiny speck with another mouthful of stew.

The top of her head promptly blew off. That was what it felt like anyway. Martha had never tasted anything like it. Her eyes bulged and streamed and her sinuses flamed and her throat seized up so she could only gasp helplessly as Lewis got up without a word and brought her back a bottle of water.

'I think I've been poisoned,' she croaked when she had downed half of it.

'I told you to be careful,' he said.

'You didn't tell me it was the culinary equivalent of an atomic bomb!' Martha felt the top of her head cautiously. It seemed to be all there but it was hard to tell.

'I've never had it,' he protested. 'But I've been offered enough chilli sauces in my time to make me very wary when I see such a little dish.'

Bully for him. Martha cast Lewis a resentful look and pushed her plate away as she gulped down more water. 'Spend six months in the Indian Ocean, I thought. It'll be perfect, I thought. Nothing but sunshine and sea and lovely fresh food. Paradise. And what do I get? A deluge and a slimy brown stew with a sauce that's destroyed my taste-buds for life!'

'The weather will improve,' said Lewis consolingly.

'Yes, but will the food? Do you think this is what Eloise cooks all the time?'

'Probably. The office manager recommended her because she lives nearby, but she never claimed to be able to do anything fancy.'

'A good meal doesn't have to be fancy,' said Martha, grateful that none of her friends were there to groan as she climbed on to her favourite hobby horse. 'The simpler the better, in fact. It's so *easy* to cook a good, nourishing meal.'

She gestured vaguely beyond the verandah. 'I mean, you'd think with all that ocean out there it wouldn't be too much to expect some fresh fish. Just grilled with a squeeze of lime, or baked with coconut, or tossed in a little butter...' Her mouth was watering at the very thought of it. 'And a nice salad on the side, and afterwards a big bowl of tropical fruit or—'

She stopped as she saw Lewis looking at her with new interest. 'What?'

'It sounds as if you can cook,' he said carefully.

'Of course I can cook!' said Martha, ruffled. What did he think? That she had spent her life shoving pre-prepared meals in the microwave? 'I love cooking. In fact, if I hadn't got into journalism, I would have— No,' she interrupted herself, belatedly realising where he was heading.

'Why not?'

'In case you've forgotten, I've got two babies to look after! I won't have time to do the cooking as well.'

'You won't have any housework, and Eloise could help you with the kids. You saw how good she was with Viola when we arrived.'

'Yes, but—'

Lewis nodded towards the pot of stew. 'And you don't *really* want to be eating this for the next six months, do you?'

Martha looked at the congealing mess. 'No,' she admitted. 'I can't say I do.'

'Why don't we renegotiate your contract?' said Lewis persuasively, pressing his advantage. 'Eloise looks after the babies while you're cooking, and she helps you feed and bath them. On top of that, you'll have no housework to do for the next six months.'

'I don't know…' Martha prevaricated.

'How about if I provide a car for you to use?'

She looked at him in surprise. 'Boy, you really don't want to eat that stew again, do you?'

'No, I don't,' he said frankly. 'You can name your terms.'

'Well, this could get interesting!' she said, lifting her eyes heavenwards as if pondering the possibilities.

'Come on, Martha. What do you say?'

Martha had already made up her mind, but she pretended to be thinking about it, just so Lewis didn't think he could push her into anything she hadn't decided for herself.

Eloise was lovely, but she clearly wasn't a cook if this meal was anything to go by. Whereas *she* liked to cook, and there was a lot to be said for doing it herself and ensuring that they all got a proper diet. She could go down to the markets and buy fruit and vegetables and fresh fish.

Martha was beginning to get excited. If Eloise would give her a hand with Noah and Viola, it would be perfect. If nothing else, cooking would make a nice change from changing nappies and wiping noses and trying to spoon food into stubborn little baby mouths, which was all her days would consist of otherwise, paradise or no paradise.

'OK,' she relented at last, and was furious at the thrill that ran through her as Lewis smiled. It was the first time she had seen him smile properly, and she was unprepared for what it did to his face. It wasn't that there was anything extraordinary about it, she tried to rationalise, alarmed by the clench of response at the base of her spine. It was just

a smile. But the light in the normally opaque slate eyes
was hard to resist and he looked so much younger, and so
much warmer.

And so much more attractive.

Enough.

Martha pushed her chair back abruptly and stood up.
'I'll get rid of this and see if I can find some fruit,' she
said.

Lewis helped her to clear the plates away. A search of
the kitchen revealed some bananas, but not much else, so
they took the bunch out to the verandah and put them on
the table between two wicker chairs.

'Oh, it's stopped raining!' Martha exclaimed as she sat
down, suddenly realising. The rain had been so thunderous
on the roof that she was astounded that she hadn't noticed
the moment it stopped.

Now the lush vegetation planted right up to the verandah
rail was bent and dripping. Insects were scraping and chir-
ruping frantically and the air was heavy with the heady
scent of damp earth and frangipani.

'Mmm…' Martha breathed it in appreciatively. 'Lovely!
Are we near the sea?'

'Everywhere is near the sea on St Bonaventure,' said
Lewis dryly. He pointed towards the end of the garden.
'See those palms?'

Martha peered into the darkness. 'Yes.'

'That's the beach there. Listen.'

He held up a finger and Martha concentrated on tuning
out the insects and the dripping, until there, very clearly
after all, was the murmur of waves breaking on to the sand.

Her face lit up. 'Oh, I *love* that sound!' She turned to
smile at Lewis. 'Things are looking up!'

'Yes, they are,' he agreed, without taking his eyes off
her face, and for some reason the breath dried in Martha's
throat as she looked back at him, imprisoned by something

new and unsettling, something that had slipped unnoticed into the atmosphere between them, tightening the air and making her heart slam inexplicably against her ribs.

When Lewis leant forward all her senses jangled and she only just stopped herself gasping, but he only pulled a banana off the bunch on the table and offered it to her.

'Have a banana,' he said softly.

'Thanks,' she croaked.

At first Martha was glad to have something to do with her hands, but she hadn't even finished peeling it before she faltered, suddenly and ridiculously awkward. She liked bananas. She had eaten thousands of them in her time. Why should eating this one seem uncomfortably suggestive?

Don't be so stupid, she told herself. It's just a banana.

But still she hesitated. Sliding a glance from under her lashes at Lewis, she saw that he was leaning forward, elbows on his knees, as he chomped his own banana thoughtfully and stared out into the darkness. *He* wasn't bothered.

Martha opened her mouth to take a bite. Of course, Lewis would choose that exact moment to look at her.

'Don't you like bananas?' he asked as she lowered hers self-consciously.

'Yes,' said Martha, horribly aware of the defensive note in her voice. Who would be *defensive* about eating a banana?

Lewis dropped his peel on to the table and helped himself to another. 'Aren't you hungry? I am. I couldn't force much of that stew down.'

'A bit.'

A *bit*? She was starving! That just made things worse.

Stupidly, Martha could feel herself blushing and was fervently grateful for the dim light that hid her pink cheeks. She hoped

She really couldn't sit holding a peeled banana like this. Any minute now, Lewis was going to ask her why she wasn't eating if she was hungry, and what was she going to tell him? That eating it in front of him suddenly seemed bizarrely erotic?

That would be an excellent conversational move on her first night alone with her new employer, wouldn't it?

Hastily, she stuffed the banana into her mouth and stared desperately at the raindrops dripping off the palm by the verandah steps as she chewed.

God, what was wrong with her tonight? It wasn't as if she was prudish or inexperienced. She was Martha Shaw, hard-bitten fashion editor. How many editorial conferences had she sat through at *Glitz* where they had all discussed sexuality from pretty much every angle, some of which she would rather not have known about, without turning a hair? Then, it had been merely a question of deciding what would most intrigue their readers, so you'd think she could manage to eat a banana now, wouldn't you?

'Another one?'

'No, thanks,' said Martha indistinctly, her mouth full. Right then she never wanted to see another banana ever again.

Lewis demolished his second. 'That's better,' he said, tossing the skin on to the table. 'I could get pretty sick of bananas, though. Do you think you could go shopping tomorrow and stock up the fridge? I'll send a car to take you.'

'Good idea,' said Martha, pathetically grateful for the change of subject. 'I'll get Eloise to show me the markets.'

Silence fell, but now that Martha had disposed of her banana it was not an awkward one. Gradually, she began to relax.

It was hot, but not oppressively so, and the scent of the night air was very intense in the humidity. Martha listened to the whirr of the insects and the soft shush of the ocean and the steady drip, drip, drip of the leaves, and felt the tension she had hardly been aware of seeping away. The babies were safe and quiet, and Lewis was still and solid beside her, and at last she could let the tiredness she had been keeping at bay trickle through her.

She needed to sleep, but the very thought of standing up was too much to contemplate. It struck Martha that she was feeling at ease for the first time in months, possibly years. There had always been so much to think about before. Her relationship with Paul, her career, coping with pregnancy on her own, adapting to having a baby, worrying about money…yes, it was a long time since she had felt this relaxed, she realised.

Lately, she had been fixated on Noah and on how she was going to get herself to St Bonaventure, but now here she was. Her body was telling her that she could stop for a while.

It was such a wonderful thought that Martha closed her eyes with a smile and stretched luxuriously, her arms above her head as a yawn escaped her. It felt good to be here.

Opening her eyes, she found Lewis looking at her with an indecipherable expression. Pinioned by his cool gaze, she could only stare back at him in mid-stretch, and the lovely relaxed feeling evaporated as her heart began to thump painfully again.

Swallowing, Martha managed to jerk her eyes away and scramble to her feet. 'I…I think I'll have a shower and go to bed,' she said nervously.

'Good idea,' said Lewis, his voice tinder-dry, and he turned back to contemplate the darkness and try not to think about her standing naked under the water. He would be taking a shower too, but his would definitely be a cold one.

* * *

When Martha woke late the next morning it took her some
time to remember where she was. She blinked up at the
ceiling fan lazily slapping the hot air above her. A chink
in the wooden blinds let a shaft of sunlight pierce the dim-
ness and cast a thin stripe across her feet.

Beside her, Viola stirred and flung out one chubby arm.
Very cautiously, so as not to wake her or Noah, sleeping
soundly on her other side, Martha eased herself upright
and pushed her dark hair back from her face. It was all
coming back to her now.

It had been a very long night. No sooner had she fallen
into a deep sleep than it seemed that the babies' body
clocks had kicked in. First Noah, then Viola had woken
up, and that had set the pattern for the night. Martha would
just get one settled when the other would start.

At one point Lewis had knocked quietly and come in to
ask if she needed help—or had she dreamed that? Martha's
brow wrinkled in an effort of memory. She had a very
vivid picture of him, barefoot and bare-chested, wearing
only a pair of loose grey pyjama bottoms.

Odd, she thought. The image had the power to disturb
her now, but at the time she couldn't remember feeling at
all awkward. She was pretty sure she had just shaken her
head and said that there was no point in two of them being
awake, as if it was quite normal for him to be half-naked
in her bedroom in the middle of the night.

Martha grimaced. She *must* have been tired!

She could certainly remember the point when she had
simply given up and taken both babies into bed with her.
There would be time enough to get them into a routine
later, she had told herself. Comforted by the warmth of
her body, Noah and Viola had quietened at last and, snug-
gling into her, they had slept like…well, babies, allowing
Martha to sink into blissful oblivion as well.

Viola's eyes suddenly snapped open and she uttered a tiny squeak.

'Oh, so you're awake, are you?' Martha picked her up and cuddled her, enjoying the feel of the small body snuffling into her. 'Shall we go and see if we can find you something to drink?'

She could hear sounds from the direction of the kitchen. Perhaps Lewis was already up? Rather to her shame, Martha found herself checking her reflection in a mirror to make sure that there was no sleep in the corner of her eyes or mascara stains under her lashes. Her hair looked dreadful, but there wasn't much she could do about that until she had a shower.

Noah was still sound asleep. Martha made sure that he was secure, and carried Viola through to the kitchen.

Lewis wasn't there, and she was cross with herself for the pang of disappointment she felt when Eloise looked up and greeted her instead. Last night she had been able to blame that kind of silliness on jet lag, but if it carried on she was going to have to get a grip.

'Have you seen Lewis yet?' she asked, trying to sound casual, as she found Viola a mug and sat her in a high chair.

Eloise nodded and told her that he had gone to the office.

'Already?' Martha looked at her wrist, but she had forgotten to put on her watch. 'What time is it?'

'Nearly eleven.'

'*Eleven?*' Aghast, she stared at Eloise. 'You should have woken me!'

'Mr Mansfield said to let you sleep,' said Eloise firmly. 'He looked in on you before he left, but you were all sleeping so soundly he didn't want to wake you.'

Hmm. Martha wasn't sure she liked the idea of Lewis

JESSICA HART   69

inspecting her while she was asleep. What if her mouth
had been open, or she'd been snoring?

Still, there was no doubt that she felt better for the rest,
and when Eloise offered to keep an eye on Viola while
she had a shower, she began to feel almost human again.
Noah was awake by then, and by the time both babies had
been fed, washed, and changed, and they had been shopping, it was not until after lunch, when they were having
a nap, that Martha had a chance to explore properly.

The house looked very different now that the dampness
and the darkness had evaporated like a bad dream.
Preoccupied with the babies' needs, it wasn't until the car
had turned up and Martha had stepped outside that she had
realised what a beautiful day it was. The sunshine and the
hot wind had sent her spirits soaring, but it was nothing
to how she felt when she pushed open the door that led
from the living area to the back verandah and walked out
to the top of the steps.

'Oh,' she said on a long breath.

This was where she had sat with Lewis the night before,
looking out into the tangled, dripping darkness and trying
to imagine it as a garden. It was very simple, with an
expanse of grass framed by luxuriant palms and exotic-
looking bushes with glossy leaves and vibrantly-coloured
flowers. A bright pink bougainvillaea scrambled along the
verandah roof and at the foot of the steps stood the frangipani tree whose intense scent Martha had smelt last
night.

Martha walked slowly down the steps and across the
grass towards the coconut palms that clustered at the end
of the garden. Their ridged trunks leant at all sorts of an-
gles, and through them she could glimpse an intense blue-
ness and the glitter of sunlight on water.

The grass gave way to coarse sand littered with coconut

husks, and then the ground dipped away and Martha found herself on a curve of white sand edging a perfect lagoon.

'Oh,' she breathed again, afraid that if she moved too suddenly or made a noise the scene would simply shimmer and disappear.

Away from the shade of the garden, it was very hot and very still. Martha slipped off her sandals and curled her toes into the soft sand with a shiver of pleasure.

Sandals dangling from one hand, she walked down to where the water was barely rippling against the beach. Shading her eyes with her hand, Martha looked out to sea. As the beach shelved away, the colour of the water intensified. Over her bare feet it was crystal clear, but it deepened imperceptibly to the palest of greens, and then to a true turquoise and at last to the deep, dark blue of the ocean beyond the reef.

Martha thought of the previous day, of how wet and gloomy it had been, and how depressed she had felt when they had arrived. It was as if she had woken up to find herself transported to an entirely different world. Walking slowly along the beach, she felt the sand warm and soft beneath her toes.

OK, she thought. I was wrong. This *is* paradise, after all.

Lewis didn't come back until nearly seven that evening. Eloise had helped Martha to give the babies a bath, but she had been long gone before the sound of a car drawing up outside sent Martha's heart lurching into her throat.

Noah and Viola were propped up against the cushions on the big sofa in the living room. Martha was alternating giving them a last bottle and trying not to wish that Lewis would come home. What could he possibly be doing all this time? she fretted. It wasn't that she was *lonely* exactly, but he really ought to think about spending some time with Viola before she went to bed.

Not that Martha could think of a way of telling Lewis that without making him think that she had missed him, and she wasn't having *that*.

So when the door opened she pretended to be absorbed in burping Noah. 'Hi,' she said over her shoulder, as casually as she could manage. Obviously that was a better option than 'Where have you been all day?' which was what she really wanted to say.

Lewis looked tired. 'I'm sorry I'm a bit late,' he said, putting his briefcase on a side table.

He must be the only person who could look crisp on a tropical island, thought Martha. It wasn't so much what he was wearing—businesslike trousers and a white short-sleeved shirt—as the way that he was wearing it, as if he would really be a lot more comfortable if he had a tie on as well, and probably a buttoned-up jacket while he was at it.

The man that fashion forgot. Martha couldn't help remembering her days at *Glitz* and how sharply the men she had met then had dressed. Most of them had been gay, of course, or serial adulterers, but still. She tried to picture Lewis at a *Glitz* party, but it involved too great a leap of the imagination. He would have been like a creature from another world.

Maybe that was how she seemed in his, thought Martha with a sudden pang, glancing down at her sleeveless top and loose trousers. It had been one of her favourite outfits the summer before last, effortlessly chic in the way only beautiful material and a designer cut could achieve.

But then she noticed the purée stains from lunch on her trousers, the crumpled collar where Viola had clutched at her with clammy little hands, the marks on her shirt where both babies had wiped their noses, and she felt strangely cheered. She wouldn't belong at a *Glitz* party either nowadays.

'It was one of those days,' Lewis said as he slumped on to the sofa next to hers. 'I meant to be home sooner.'

'It doesn't matter.' Martha was carefully unconcerned. 'What time is it, anyway?'

As if she hadn't been looking at her watch every five minutes for the last three hours.

Lewis looked at his watch. 'Six minutes to seven.'

'Couldn't you be a bit more precise?' she asked ironically.

'Sorry. I've been dealing with details all day, and you get into the habit after a while.' Martha just looked at him and, after a moment, Lewis gave in and laughed. 'OK, so I'm precise. What can I say? I'm an engineer.'

'I thought so.' Martha smiled and put Noah down so that she could give Viola the last of her bottle.

Lewis watched her feeding the baby for a while. 'So, how has your day been?' he asked at last.

'Fine,' she said, her eyes on Viola. 'It's a beautiful place, isn't it? I took Viola and Noah down to the beach for a paddle and they loved the water, but it was really too hot for them. I had to bring them back into the shade after a few minutes. And we went shopping, of course. Thanks for sending the car, by the way. It would have been a long way to walk back with all the stuff.'

'That sounds promising,' said Lewis. 'No more okra stew tonight, then?'

'No. Eloise is delighted that she doesn't have to do the cooking.'

'So I gathered,' he said. 'She practically fell on my neck when I suggested the alternative arrangements. Do you think it will work out?'

'I'm sure it will,' said Martha. 'Of course, it'll be better when we get into a routine.' She turned her attention back to Viola. 'We had a very late start this morning, as you probably know.'

Lewis shrugged, wishing he could shrug off the memory of how she had looked when he had quietly opened her door that morning. She had obviously been too hot in the night and was lying half in and half out of the top sheet, wearing what looked like a man's shirt, which exposed rather more of her legs than she had probably realised.

Averting his gaze, Lewis had spotted Noah and Viola tucked on either side of her. All three of them had been sound asleep. Martha's face had been pressed into the pillow, while the ceiling fan gently stirred her dark hair.

His throat was ridiculously dry for some reason, and he cleared it self-consciously. How could you have a dry throat in this humidity? 'You must have been tired,' he said. 'The babies seemed to be awake most of the night.'

She looked up at him abruptly, her brown eyes very clear and direct. 'Did you come in at one point?' she asked.

'I thought you might need some help,' he said, inexplicably defensive. 'I'm sorry, I did knock, but you obviously couldn't hear. Would you rather I didn't in future?'

'No,' said Martha hastily, and to Lewis's surprise she seemed even more awkward than he did. 'I...I just wondered if I had dreamt it or not, that's all.'

'No,' he said. 'You didn't dream it.'

They looked at each other and the silence strummed between them. For Martha, it was as if she were back in the dimly lit room. Lewis was there, with his bare chest and his bare feet, and she was in an old grandad shirt and nothing else. She had taken to sleeping in it since Noah was born. It was very soft fine cotton in a blue that had faded in washing until it was almost white and came a decent way down her thighs if she didn't bend over too far.

Martha's skin prickled as if she could feel its cool softness against her now, and she was suddenly aware of how naked she had been beneath it in a way she hadn't been the night before. It would have been so easy to have touched Lewis, to have rested her palm against his chest or run her hand down his flank, and what would have happened then? The mere thought was enough to dry the breath in her throat.

With an effort, she dragged her mind back to the present. 'I mean, I don't want you to feel that you need to offer to help,' she said awkwardly. 'You're paying me to be the one who gets up in the middle of the night if Viola is crying.'

Yes, and it might be an idea if she remembered that, Martha reminded herself sternly. She was a nanny and Lewis was her employer, and don't forget it.

Lewis was rubbing the back of his neck tiredly. 'That's the trouble with babies,' he said. 'They make everything so...' he trailed off, searching for the right word '...so *intimate*,' he decided at last. 'You think you'll just hire a nanny to look after the baby, and before you know where you are you're sharing the small hours with a stranger and you're both half naked.'

So he had been thinking about how very few clothes they had on between them too. Martha didn't know whether to be glad or sorry about that.

Take it lightly, anyway, she told herself.

'Hopefully they'll settle into a routine soon, and they won't wake up in the night,' she said, really quite pleased with her careless tone. 'And then there won't be any need for either of us to wander around half naked!'

Viola had come to the end of her bottle, so she sat her up and patted her gently on the back. 'She's a gorgeous baby, isn't she?' said Martha, deciding that it was high time they changed the subject. She turned Viola to face her, holding the baby between her hands so that she could admire her fierce blue eyes and rosebud mouth. 'And don't you know it?' she said to her with a smile.

Viola eyed her consideringly for a moment before responding with an almighty belch so at odds with her daintiness that Martha and Lewis couldn't help laughing.

'That's my girl!' said Lewis, and Viola beamed, not understanding how she had banished the simmering tension in the atmosphere but delighted with their reaction. She held out her arms to her uncle in an unmistakable gesture.

'Do you want to take her?' Martha asked, and Lewis instantly looked alarmed.

'To do what?'

'Don't panic, there's no nappy changing required! Just give her a bit of a cuddle.' Martha deposited Viola in his arms before he had time to think up any objections. 'Look, here's a book,' she said, handing him a board book with bright simple images. 'Read that with her.'

Lewis did his best, but the fact was that Viola wasn't the slightest bit interested in the book. It was more fun to explore her uncle's face with inquisitive little fingers, sticking them in his mouth, patting his nose, tugging at his lips and pulling at his hair until he winced.

'Why won't she sit quietly like him?' he complained, casting an envious glance to where Noah was sitting angelically on his mother's lap, responding suitably with coos and gurgles as she turned the pages.

'I can't imagine.' Martha's lips were pressed together in an effort to stop herself laughing at Lewis's struggles to distract his small niece. 'I think you might find there's some very contrary family genes in Viola!'

'More than likely,' said Lewis glumly, thinking of his sister.

'Just wait until she's old enough to answer back!'

He grimaced. At eight months, the strength of Viola's

character was already obvious. God only knew what she would be like once she started to talk.

'She's going to need a very firm hand,' said Martha, reading his expression without difficulty.

'That'll be her parents' problem,' said Lewis, removing Viola's finger from his ear. 'It's nothing to do with me.'

Even to himself that had the ring of famous last words.

CHAPTER FIVE

MARTHA took pity on him at last and took a protesting Viola away to bed. 'I think she likes you,' she told Lewis as Viola set up a wail at being separated from her newest plaything.

Rubbing his nose tenderly, where the tiny fingers had pinched, Lewis wasn't sure that he wanted to hear that.

Both babies went down with suspicious ease. 'Quick,' said Martha, closing the door on them. 'Let's eat before they start.'

She had made a fresh salsa to go with some grilled fish, a simple but effective meal that made Lewis eye her with new appreciation. 'I'm beginning to think it was lucky that Eve fell in love after all,' he said.

Was that a subtle way of reminding her that she wasn't his first choice? Martha wondered. 'Thank you…I think!'

But the truth was that she was glad Eve had fallen in love too. If she hadn't, she would be here in this beautiful place, and when Lewis offered to clear up she was even gladder. 'You go and sit down,' he said. 'I'll bring you some coffee.'

There was no doubt that it was nice to be looked after for a change. Martha sat on the verandah and let herself relax. There was a breeze tonight, and she could hear the sea beyond the rustling palms, while from behind her came the sound of Lewis moving around the kitchen. It was oddly comforting to know that he was in there and would be coming out to join her any minute now.

Not that she was waiting for him or anything.

Although, if she wasn't waiting, why did her heart

clutch in that disturbing way as Lewis slid open the door on to the verandah and put a mug on the table next to her?

Suppressing it firmly, Martha thanked him with studied nonchalance. It was no big deal. He had only made coffee, and he had just happened to choose to sit on the chair beside hers. That wasn't a big deal either. He could hardly go and sit at the other end of the verandah, could he? That would look rude.

Lewis leant back with a sigh and closed his eyes. He did look tired, thought Martha, conscious of an alarming impulse to smooth the hair back from his forehead. The soft light from the lamps in the living room behind her spilled out through the sliding glass doors and lit the severe profile.

Martha's gaze drifted along the strong line of cheek and jaw to rest at the edge of that stern mouth where it faltered for a moment as she found herself remembering how it changed when he smiled. There was something intriguing about the way a mouth that looked cool could be transformed in an instant into warmth by the mere stretching of the muscles in his cheeks.

If a smile could have such a dramatic effect, what would a kiss do to it? Lewis seemed so reserved and self-contained, it was hard to imagine him as a lover...or maybe not, thought Martha, her eyes still on his mouth, and a queer feeling stirred inside her as a vivid picture sprang to mind of Lewis smiling, reaching for her, pulling her towards him, of how firm his hands would be on her, of how warm and exciting his lips would feel against hers...

Sucking in her breath, Martha wrenched her gaze away, aghast at how clearly she could imagine it, and at the way the mere thought of his mouth had triggered a tiny trembling just beneath her skin. What was she *doing*?

She sipped her coffee with a kind of desperation. *Stop it*, she told herself fiercely. Just be normal.

'Busy day?' she asked, wincing at the way her voice seemed to loop up and down, as if she really had kissed him.

Lewis opened his eyes and turned his head to look at her. 'More frustrating than busy,' he said. 'It always takes longer than you anticipate to get everything sorted out and everyone in the right place at the right time with the right equipment.'

'You don't just mix up your concrete and start pouring then?'

Lewis stared at her as if he couldn't decide whether she was joking or not.

'Do you know what's involved in setting up a fashion shoot?' said Martha with a shade of defiance.

'No.'

'Well, then.'

His expression relaxed slightly. 'OK,' he said, acknowledging the point with a half smile. 'So, no, we're not in a position to start pouring concrete yet. We won't be doing that for another fifteen months or so.'

'Fifteen *months*? That's over a year!'

Excellent, Martha, she thought, cringing inwardly at her own fatuous comment. Nothing like stating the obvious.

But she was terrified of what she might be tempted to do if they just sat in silence, so she had to keep him talking. Anything was better than sitting there and wondering about his mouth and how it would feel…

She cleared her throat. 'Why does it take so long before you can start building?'

'Why this sudden interest in the construction process?' asked Lewis a little suspiciously. He wouldn't have thought Martha was the type to be riveted by the nitty-gritty of civil engineering.

'I was just making conversation,' she said, a little ruffled. 'Besides, we're going to be spending the next six months together, so I might as well understand what you're going to be doing all day.'

Luckily, Lewis seemed to accept that. He started talking about feasibility studies and exploratory surveys, not much of which Martha understood, but she brightened when he mentioned the specialists who would be coming out to do the topographical and hydrological surveys and a detailed economic analysis.

'I may need to do some entertaining when they all arrive,' he said. 'Would you be able to cope with that, or should I ask around about someone who could cater?'

'No, I could do it,' said Martha quickly, thinking that if she was going to feel as self-conscious as this with him every evening, the more people who were around the better. 'I'd like to do it, in fact. I enjoy making special meals, and it would be great to meet some new people.'

She had only been here a day, thought Lewis, a little disgruntled. Wasn't it a bit soon for her to be craving a social life?

'Well…good,' he said, wishing he could sound as enthusiastic as she did at the prospect.

There was a short silence. Martha was suddenly acutely aware of the suck and sigh of the waves breaking on the shore, and the whispering of the palms as they swayed in the warm breeze.

And of Lewis sitting so still and self-contained beside her.

The silence was beginning to stretch uncomfortably. 'Go on with what you were saying about preliminary design,' she said with an edge of desperation.

She wondered if Lewis had been as aware of the silence as she had been. He certainly seemed grateful for the cue, and plunged back into an explanation of what was in-

volved in designing and constructing two major projects
simultaneously.

Most of it went over Martha's head, but it was easier to
watch him when he was talking and she liked to see the
austere face animated. All she needed to do was prompt
him every now and then.

'What's an EIA again?' she asked, confused by the
plethora of initials and acronyms.

'An Environmental Impact Assessment,' said Lewis,
well into his stride by now. He was feeling better. The
silence and the darkness and Martha's deep eyes unsettled
him. It was easier to concentrate on talking about the project. He knew where he was with that.

'The World Bank require us to complete detailed studies
about the impact any construction will have on the local
habitat before funding goes ahead. So we'll get in a botanist to look at the airport site, and a marine biologist
who's familiar with these waters to survey the port. We're
going to have to dig a deep trench for ships and that can
have an effect on bigger fish like sharks and—' He
stopped, realising that Martha had straightened with new
attention. 'What?'

'Did you say you would be needing a marine biologist?'
Martha asked, feeling terrible that she had hardly given
Rory a thought since she had arrived. The whole purpose
of being here was to find him, and it had taken Lewis's
casual mention of a marine biologist to remind her about
him at all.

'What about it?' said Lewis, but with foreboding. Even
as he said the words he knew that she was going to bring
up Noah's father. Sure enough, her response came bang
on cue.

'Rory's a marine biologist specialising in this part of the
ocean.'

Lewis frowned. It had been a long day and he had just

been starting to relax after the excellent meal Martha had cooked. He had got used to solitary evenings after Helen had left, and it had been nice to sit on the verandah and talk at the end of the day for a change. For a minute there he had forgotten just what Martha was doing in St Bonaventure, but she clearly hadn't.

'These are important projects,' he said crossly, knowing that he couldn't really justify his bad temper but unable to do anything about it. 'I can't run around dishing out jobs to any old Tom, Dick and Harry because he happens to be my nanny's boyfriend.'

Martha flushed with annoyance. 'It wouldn't occur to me to ask you to give Rory a job,' she snapped. 'I just thought that you might come across someone who would know him because they work in the same field.'

'It's possible,' Lewis allowed, knowing that it was more than likely. There weren't that many marine biologists qualified to do the EIA at the port, and it would be a small and specialised world.

'Well, when you do appoint a biologist, perhaps you could ask them if they know Rory,' she said, her voice cold. She didn't understand why Lewis was suddenly so grumpy.

'If I remember, and if an opportunity comes up,' he said grudgingly, 'but frankly I've got better things to do than track down your boyfriends for you! In any case, I won't be dealing with the marine survey immediately,' he went on while Martha was still struggling to frame a suitably crushing retort. 'There's plenty to do before we get round to finding a marine biologist.'

'In that case I'd better *track Rory down*, as you put it, myself,' said Martha tightly. 'It can't be that hard on an island this size.'

'I imagine not,' said Lewis in a frosty voice. 'It's no business of mine what you choose to do in your free time, but I'd be grateful if you'd remember that you're here primarily to look after my niece. I don't want her abandoned with Eloise while you chase after marine biologists.'

Tight-lipped, Martha got to her feet. How dared he suggest she would ignore Viola? 'Don't worry, I won't forget,' she said between clenched teeth, and headed inside before she really lost her temper and started telling her employer exactly what she thought about him.

Why had she mentioned Rory? They had been having a nice evening until then. A bit tense at times, perhaps, but not in a bad way. More in an intriguing, secretly exciting type of way. The kind of way that made you very aware of the scent of flowers and the sound of the sea and the warm breeze against your skin. That made you think about your employer in a way you really shouldn't be thinking about him.

Martha kicked off the sheet irritably. It was too hot, and she hadn't been sleepy, anyway, but there was nowhere else to go but bed. Perhaps it was just as well Lewis had been so disagreeable about Rory, she tried to console herself. It had reminded her that at heart he was just as cold and unpleasant as he had seemed that first day she had met him in London.

There had been no need for him to jump down her throat like that. It was outrageous to suggest that she would neglect Viola. And it wasn't as if she hadn't made it very clear why she wanted to come to St Bonaventure. Anyone would think from the way he had carried on that she had demanded that he produce Rory on a plate for her!

Well, he needn't worry, Martha vowed fiercely. She didn't need Lewis's help. She would be the perfect nanny *and* she would find Rory by herself, and that would show him!

Restlessly, she punched her pillow into shape and threw herself back down, only for it to occur to her that wanting to prove her point to Lewis Mansfield was not the best of reasons for wanting to find Rory. She was supposed to be thinking about Noah's need for a father, not about Lewis.

And she *was*, Martha insisted to herself. It was just that she wanted to show Lewis too.

The next morning, she was determinedly cool. At least her early night had got her back into a more normal routine, and by seven she was in the kitchen with both babies installed in high chairs. None of them were dressed, but you couldn't have everything. Barefoot and wearing her old shirt, Martha had put some coffee on and was getting Viola and Noah a drink when Lewis came in.

'Good morning,' she said, frigidly polite and trying not to notice how crisp and cool he looked. It made her very conscious of her crumpled shirt and unwashed face. Surreptitiously, she wiped under her eyes and pushed her tousled hair behind her ears in an effort to disguise the fact that it was going in all directions.

'Would you like some breakfast?' she asked, the perfect servant.

'I'll just make myself some coffee, thanks.' Lewis seemed a bit disconcerted to find her there.

'There's some in the pot there.' Delighted to be able to demonstrate her efficiency, Martha nodded her head in the direction of the stove and, after a moment's hesitation Lewis went over and poured himself a mug.

Leaning against the counter, he watched her give Viola a two-handled mug and screw the top firmly on to Noah's. She was wearing that shirt again, the one that hung cool and loose and left her legs bare. It didn't cling, and it wasn't transparent or seductive in any way, but every time Lewis looked at it he couldn't help thinking about the fact that she was almost certainly naked underneath.

He made himself concentrate on his coffee instead. 'Look, I'm sorry about last night,' he said abruptly.

Martha looked up from Noah's mug. 'Last night?' she echoed cautiously.

'I could have been more understanding about the fact that you want to find Noah's father.'

Lewis had done some thinking after she had stalked off to bed, and he didn't feel good about the way he had behaved. He had tried telling himself that he was just being protective of Viola and afraid that Martha would simply forget about staying six months when she found Rory, but he had a nasty feeling that he had ended up sounding jealous instead.

'You made it clear that's why you were here,' he persevered, determined to get it all off his chest, 'and we came to an agreement on that basis. It'll be difficult for you to find out much in your free time, with so many places closed on a Sunday, so I just wanted you to know that I will ask around for you and let you know if I hear any news of Rory.'

Martha stared at him, thrown and more than a little frustrated. What was he doing apologising and being nice? If he was going to be totally unreasonable, the way he had been last night, it would really be better if he just stayed that way and then she would know where she was. As it was, she had no sooner fired herself up with a determination to prove him wrong than he had to go and deflate her by offering to find Rory himself. Really, it was almost perverse of him. She could hardly refuse to accept his help, though, could she?

'Oh…well…thank you,' she said awkwardly, not knowing what else she could say.

'It might not be immediately,' he warned, 'but I'll find out what I can.'

'No, that's OK, honestly. There's no hurry. I've got six months, after all.'

'Good.' Back to his usual brisk self, Lewis swallowed the last of his coffee in a gulp. 'I'd better go.'

He put his mug in the sink and headed for the door, only to turn at the last moment. 'By the way, nice shirt,' he said, straight-faced, and then he was gone, leaving Martha standing in the middle of the kitchen, still clutching Noah's mug.

Thirsty, and despairing of his mother ever noticing him while she had that funny expression on her face, Noah let out an indignant squawk. It had the desired effect. Martha started and handed him the mug, although with something less than her usual degree of attention. She was looking down at her bare legs instead and remembering the expression in Lewis's eyes as they rested on them.

Nice shirt? she was thinking, and the faintest of smiles curled her lips.

After the first week Martha felt as if she had been on St Bonaventure for ever. It had taken no time at all to fall into a routine and, with Eloise to help the sun-drenched days blended one into another. Her once chic wardrobe was reduced to a sleeveless T-shirt and a sarong, and her frenetic days in the *Glitz* office to a simpler, slower routine of shopping in the market, cooking, chatting to Eloise in the kitchen, and playing with Noah and Viola.

Some days she would put big floppy hats on their heads and take them down to the beach. Noah loved the water and would sit happily splashing in the lagoon for as long as Martha would let him stay in the sun, but Viola—typically—was more fastidious, and protested loudly if her hands got too sticky with sand.

It was often easier to let them both sit on a rug in the shade of the verandah. Martha never got tired of watching the wonder in their faces as they explored each new sensation. Savannah had sent out a ridiculous number of expensive toys for Viola, but she didn't need any of them. A battered saucepan or an empty plastic bottle to bang on the ground provided entertainment enough.

Martha felt calmer and more relaxed than she had in years, she realised, sitting in the tattered shade of the palms with the 'twins', as she had started to call them, asleep on a rug beside her. She had loved the frenetic life at *Glitz*, the gossip and the parties and the tantrums and the adrenalin rush of constant deadlines, but it seemed to belong to a parallel universe now, where a girl who looked just like her had splurged money on shoes and handbags and the latest must-have accessories without a thought for the future.

It was odd to be able to remember it all so clearly and yet feel as if the memories belonged to someone else entirely. She had had a wonderful time, that was for sure, but she didn't miss any of it.

How could she miss anything when she was in paradise? Martha wondered, watching a cat's paw of wind shiver across the lagoon.

Only…if this was paradise, why wasn't she completely happy?

She was getting paid to live in this beautiful place. The babies were gorgeous and blooming. All things considered, she had a pretty easy life.

It was just that sometimes she felt…Martha's brow furrowed as she sought for the right word…felt a little, well, *lonely*. Which was ridiculous when she had Eloise to talk to all day, and the fishermen and market traders to banter with when she went shopping.

And, in the evenings, there was Lewis.

Martha didn't like the way she looked forward to his return every day, or the way the dreamlike state in which she spent her days snapped into something more vivid the moment he walked through the door. It made her feel edgy and unsettled, as if she somehow wasn't quite complete until he was there.

It wasn't even as if Lewis made any particular effort to turn on the charm. Far from it. He was austere and often brusque, and there was an acid edge to his tongue at times. His logical approach to everything drove Martha mad, and they argued hotly at times. At least, *she* argued hotly. Lewis just sat there and infuriated her by being practical and rational and thinking things through before he opened his mouth.

So why did she start listening for his car at six o'clock, and why did a tiny thrill shiver down her spine as soon as he appeared?

She needed to meet more people, Martha decided. Make her life bigger. Wasn't that what the agony aunt at *Glitz* always said to readers? If she made the effort to get out more and develop a social life of her own, she wouldn't be so dependent on Lewis.

She ought to make an effort to find Rory too. And she would…just as soon as she had found her feet.

It was hard to get up the energy to make the effort, though, when the days blended into each other in a haze of sunshine and shushing waves and soft breezes. And when Lewis asked her that morning if she had any plans for the day, Martha could only look at him in surprise.

'Plans? No. Should I have?'

'It's Sunday,' he said. 'Your day off.'

'Oh.' How could you have a day off in paradise? Martha wondered.

'I thought you might like some time to yourself,' said Lewis. 'You could have the car, if you like. Take Noah with you, or leave him with me and Viola. It's up to you.'

'Well…I hadn't really thought,' she said uncertainly. Shouldn't the thought of a day on her own be more appealing? 'The thing is, I wouldn't want to leave Noah, but

I don't think it's a good idea to split him and Viola up just when they're getting used to being together all the time.'

It was a pretty lame excuse, but Lewis seemed to fall for it.

'In that case, perhaps you'd like to go out to lunch?' he suggested. 'The office manager was telling me about a restaurant on the other side of the island. I gather it's not much more than a shack, but the fish is supposed to be excellent, and it's right on the beach so the twins aren't likely to be a problem.'

Martha liked the way he had started calling Noah and Viola the 'twins' without thinking about it.

'If nothing else, it would make a change for you if someone else did the cooking,' he said.

The trouble with Lewis was that it was impossible to tell what he was thinking most of the time. Was that austere air a cover for the fact that he really wanted to take her out to lunch, or was he just being polite?

And did it really matter? Martha asked herself. She wanted to go, whatever his reason for asking her, and there was no point in pretending that she didn't.

'That sounds wonderful,' she said. 'Thank you.'

'It's the least I can do after you've saved me from Eloise's okra stew,' he said gruffly. 'Bring a swimming costume. The water is deeper there and I'm told it's better for swimming.'

The office manager hadn't been exaggerating when he had said that the restaurant wasn't much more than a shack. Open on one side, its walls were cobbled together with a mixture of wood and tin, and the menu was scrawled on a bleached piece of driftwood, but the tables were set out under a shade made from woven palm leaves, the beer miraculously cold, and the fish the freshest Martha had ever seen.

'And it comes with built-in babysitters,' she said to Lewis as Viola and Noah were swept off by a group of women sitting at the next table who exclaimed over their fairness and insisted on looking after them. Noah was a bit doubtful at first, but Viola loved the attention, and after a while he succumbed and stopped looking over his shoulder for his mother.

'Your niece is a terrible flirt,' Martha said with mock severity. 'Look at the way she's batting her eyelashes and just revelling in the attention! I wish I had half her technique!'

Lewis looked across the table at Martha. She was smiling as she watched the women with the two babies. She had been careful not to get burnt, but a week in the sun had given her a glow. She had put on some weight, too, and in her sleeveless T-shirt and carelessly tied sarong she looked like another woman entirely from the one who had walked into his office that day.

Lewis's eyes dwelt on her face as he tried to work out where the difference lay. She wasn't classically beautiful, and without make-up he could see the fine lines around her eyes that betrayed her age. Her nose was too big and her mouth too wide for prettiness, but now that the chic, brittle air had vanished she looked relaxed and somehow much more appealing. She had grown familiar to him, too, he realised. It was as if he had always known the exact colour of her eyes, the tilt of her lashes, the way she pushed her hair behind her ears or smiled as she picked up a baby.

'I can't believe your technique ever needed any improvement,' he said without thinking, and Martha glanced at him.

'You'd be surprised,' she said ironically, thinking of some of her more unsatisfactory relationships. 'I certainly never had Viola's ability to twist perfect strangers round her little finger. She's going to be a force to be reckoned with when she grows up. I've never met a baby with so much character!'

Lewis looked at his niece, chortling and gurgling to the accompaniment of much cooing. 'Too much character sometimes,' he said in a dry voice. 'Noah is much more easygoing. I've been hoping his laid-back approach will rub off on Viola.'

'I doubt it,' said Martha, eyeing her small son fondly. 'He's just like his father—laid back and chilled out.'

'Can you really tell who he's like at this stage?' Lewis was unaccountably ruffled by the affection in her voice.

'Well, he's certainly not like me. I can't see any physical resemblance,' she admitted, 'but in temperament Noah is just like Rory. Rory was always incredibly easygoing too. When you're used to dealing with prima donnas all day it's incredibly refreshing to come across someone with such a sweet temper. He never needed anyone to dance attendance upon him or flatter him or tell him he was wonderful. He just lay back and let life wash over him.'

'Isn't that just another way of saying that he was completely passive?' said Lewis in a hard voice.

Martha frowned slightly and thought about it as she drank her beer. 'I don't think he was *passive*, exactly,' she said after a moment. 'I think it was more a sort of laziness. Rory never had to make much of an effort because he was so nice and so good-looking that people came to him. He's never going to make a fortune, but he'll probably have a good time, and there's a lot to be said for that.'

'Yes, it's a great life if you can get everyone else to do your dirty work for you,' Lewis agreed. 'All you've got to do is turn on the charm and let all those boring, sensible people take decisions and be responsible while you just get on with being laid-back and relaxed and at one with yourself.'

The unmistakable bitterness lacing his voice made Martha look at him curiously. 'It sounds like you're thinking of someone in particular,' she said. 'Your sister?'

'Savannah?' Lewis gave a mirthless laugh. 'No, she's certainly irresponsible, but if there's one thing you can't call Savannah it's "laid-back"!'

'Who, then?'

'I was thinking about my mother,' he admitted after a momentary hesitation. 'She's never been one to burden herself with responsibilities.'

'I didn't realise you had a mother,' said Martha without thinking.

'What, did you think I came into this world wearing a suit and tie?' he asked sardonically.

'Of course not,' she said, feeling a fool. 'Though, come to think of it, it's hard to imagine you as a little boy. What were you like?'

'Just the way I am now, I expect, but shorter.'

Martha gave him an old-fashioned look, and picked up her beer once more. 'You've never mentioned your mother before.'

'She's not a big part of my life.' He shrugged. 'She certainly didn't feature much in my childhood. It didn't take her long to get bored of marriage and motherhood, but I suppose she lasted longer than Savannah's mother, at least. I was about six when she left.'

Six? Martha couldn't believe a mother would walk out on a six-year-old. 'Why did she leave?'

'She wanted to "find herself".' Lewis hooked his fingers to add ironic quotation marks around the phrase. 'She's still searching, as far as I know,' he added dryly.

'Is she still alive?'

'Oh, yes. She drifts around the world pleasantly enough, I think. She's the kind of person who thinks it's oppressive to live in a house. She's always in some ashram, or tepee, or tribal longhouse, chanting about peace and love.'

Lewis took a pull of his beer and stared out at the sea glittering beyond the palm shade. 'She's not insincere. I think she probably really believes that if she stands on her head for a month, or only eats seaweed, that the world will change, but of course it doesn't. You'd think she'd get cynical after a while, but she never does.'

'Do you ever see her?'

'Occasionally. It's hard to think of her as a mother, really. She's just an eccentric stranger who turns up every now and then and enthuses about the latest alternative therapy that prevents her facing up to her own responsibilities.'

Martha looked across at the other table, where Noah was being cuddled against an ample bosom, and she shuddered. She couldn't bear the thought of him describing her as an eccentric stranger a few years down the line. But then, she couldn't imagine ever leaving him.

Her heart cracked at the thought of Lewis, aged six, left behind while his mother went off to find something more interesting to do, and her fingers curled in her lap. It wasn't surprising that he had a jaundiced view of women with the example he had been set by the women in his own family.

She glanced at him from under her lashes. He was watching the sea, his mouth set in a grim line, and she sensed that he was revisiting some unhappy memories.

'I always wanted to be laid-back, but I was never very good at it,' she said to lighten the tone. 'I was a terrible swot at school, and very ambitious. I always knew that I wanted to work on a magazine, and I loved my job, but after a while it just took over my life. You're always looking over your shoulder at the others coming behind you, and you know that if you mess up just once you'll be stabbed to death by all the stilettos trampling over you while you're down.'

Lewis had turned to listen to her, and she was glad to see that the bitterness had gone from his face. 'You can't afford to relax when you're under that kind of pressure. You spend your whole life running on adrenalin, because that's the only way you're going to make the next party, the next deadline, the next edition, the next season's looks.'

She shook her head, remembering. 'When I think about it now, I was permanently tense. It's not good to live like that.'

Lewis's eyes rested on her. 'You've changed,' he said.

CHAPTER SIX

MARTHA smiled reluctantly. 'Noah has changed me,' she said. 'I wouldn't have changed by myself, I don't think. I never have had the time to think about what I might want to change into,' she added thoughtfully. 'It's not always a bad thing to slow down, and it's not the same as opting out completely.'

'No, I know.'

'I don't regret it for a moment,' she went on, her eyes on Noah, 'but for a time there after Noah was born it was really scary. I felt as if my entire life was unravelling. One minute I had a great social life, a fantastic job, and lots of money, and the next it seemed as if it had all gone. I hadn't realised how interconnected they all were. When one fell apart, the others did too.'

She grimaced at the memory of how lonely it had been. Most of her friends had worked for *Glitz*, so as soon as she lost her job she had been out of the gossip loop, and that was fatal.

It wasn't that anyone had deliberately dropped her, but the fact was that they were all living the free-wheeling life she had enjoyed for so long, and she just didn't fit into it any more. They worked hard and they played hard, and they didn't have children to go home to. They could afford to go out and enjoy themselves, and had the stamina to stay out all night, just as she had once done.

'It's frightening how quickly everything gets out of control,' she confessed to Lewis. 'Slowing down is fantastic in a place like this—' gesturing at the idyllic beach in front of them '—but when you've slowed right down in an expensive city with no money and all your friends are busy with careers and there's no one to help you with your new baby, it's not so much fun.

'That's why I'm really grateful to you for giving me this job.' Martha turned back to smile at Lewis. 'If I hadn't had this chance to unwind I'm not sure how much longer I could have gone on without snapping. I've only been here a week and already I feel like a completely different person.' She let out a long sigh. 'Thank you,' she said simply.

'There's no need to thank me,' said Lewis gruffly, averting his eyes from her smile. 'You're doing a good job.'

He stared at the bay, wondering how he could look at the water and see only her smile shimmering in front of his eyes.

'I just hope you'll feel the same in six months' time,' he said.

'I think I will,' said Martha.

'Will you? You've talked about the kind of life you used to have, hectic work, frenetic social life, always on the go…you don't think there's a danger that you'll get bored here after a while?'

Not if you're here too. The words hovered on Martha's tongue, springing there so immediately that for an awful moment she thought she had actually said them aloud.

And how would she explain *that*?

She stared out as Lewis had done, beyond the tatty shade to the glare of the white sand and the glittering water. She was suddenly, intensely conscious of the cold beer in her hand, of the press of the rickety wooden chair underneath her thighs, and the smell and sizzle of fish being cooked in the shack behind her. The chatter of the women at the next table had faded to a background murmur, and there was only Lewis, sitting still and solid and somehow, suddenly, sexy as hell.

The Harlequin Reader Service® — Here's how it works:

If offer card is missing write to: Harlequin Reader Service, 3010 Walden Ave., P.O. Box 1867, Buffalo NY 14240-1867

NO POSTAGE
NECESSARY
IF MAILED
IN THE
UNITED STATES

BUSINESS REPLY MAIL

FIRST-CLASS MAIL   PERMIT NO. 717-003   BUFFALO, NY

POSTAGE WILL BE PAID BY ADDRESSEE

HARLEQUIN READER SERVICE
3010 WALDEN AVE
PO BOX 1867
BUFFALO NY 14240-9952

Play the
Lucky
Hearts
Game

and get...

2 FREE BOOKS
and a FREE MYSTERY GIFT...

Yes! YOURS to KEEP!

**I have scratched off the silver card.
Please send me my 2 FREE BOOKS and
FREE mystery GIFT. I understand that I am
under no obligation to purchase any books as
explained on the back of this card.**

Scratch Here!

then look below to see
what your cards get you...
2 Free Books & a Free
Mystery Gift!

▶ DETACH AND MAIL CARD TODAY! ▶

386 HDL DZ5V   186 HDL DZ6C

FIRST NAME	LAST NAME

ADDRESS

APT.#	CITY

STATE/PROV.	ZIP/POSTAL CODE

(H-R-05/04)

Twenty-one gets you
2 FREE BOOKS
and a **FREE MYSTERY GIFT!**

Twenty gets you
2 FREE BOOKS!

Nineteen gets you
1 FREE BOOK!

TRY AGAIN!

Offer limited to one per household and not valid to current Harlequin Romance® subscribers. All orders subject to approval.

© 2002 HARLEQUIN ENTERPRISES LTD. ® and TM are trademarks owned by Harlequin Enterprises Ltd

Uh-oh.

'I...er...I probably do need to make more of an effort
to meet people,' she said. 'We've been settling in this
week, but now that we've got a routine I can find out if
there's anything like a mother and baby group in
Perpetua.' Martha tried to sound enthusiastic about the
prospect.

'I was thinking more about you needing some adult
company,' said Lewis. 'Leave the twins with Eloise one
day, and come and have lunch in town. I'll introduce you
to some people.'

Martha glanced at him uncertainly. Why was he so keen
for her to expand her social life? What if he was afraid
that *he* was one who would be bored with just her for
company for the next six months? Was that what she had
come to? Martha Shaw, social burden?

She cringed at the very thought. Well, Lewis needn't
worry if that was the case. It ought to be easy enough to
show him that she wasn't the needy type, and had no intention of hanging around the house all day waiting for
him to come home.

The way she had been doing all week, in fact.

That was all going to change. 'Would you really?' she
said brightly. 'That sounds fantastic! I'd love to meet some
new people.'

Lewis looked a bit taken aback by her show of eager-
ness, but he nodded. 'I'll let you know,' he said.

Reclaiming the two babies from the neighbouring table,
they fed them on their laps before their own meals arrived.
It was so much easier when there were two of you, Martha
thought.

Of course, Eloise was usually there to help, but it was
different with Lewis. Martha couldn't quite think of a good
reason why it should be so, she just knew that it was.

She looked across the table. Lewis had Noah on his lap,

and was giving him a piece of banana that he had just retrieved from his shirt. The strong nose wrinkled fastidiously at the mess Noah had made of it already, but when he glanced up and caught Martha's eye he grinned, and the breath snared in her throat as something shifted dangerously inside her.

'Disgusting, aren't they?' he said, and she managed to tear her eyes away.

'Revolting,' she agreed shakily.

Afterwards, the babies slept in the shade while Martha and Lewis ate lunch. The fish was as delicious as promised, but Martha couldn't concentrate on the meal. She was terribly aware of Lewis, for some reason, and nervous of the silence that fell whenever she looked at him and thought about his hands and his mouth, and wondered what it would feel like if she could reach across and run her fingers along the strong forearm, down over the soft, dark hairs to the broad wrist and the back of his hand, what it would be like to be able to lace her fingers between his and turn his hand over and lift his palm to her mouth...

Gulping, she made herself talk brightly instead, and whenever a pause loomed she asked him another question about the project, and the firm, and how he had set it up with a friend three years ago.

'We've got a very small staff at the moment,' Lewis told her, a bit wary of her almost feverish interest but deciding it was easier to answer than to probe as to why she was suddenly acting so nervous. 'We have resident engineers on each site, but otherwise we employ freelance specialists, and I move between sites just to keep an eye on things or, like now, get the project up and running.'

'It must mean a lot of travelling for you.'

'It makes sense for me to do it. Mike is married and he's got a young family, so he stays in London and runs our head office. I don't have any commitments so I'm much more flexible.'

'Don't you ever get tired of it?' she asked.

'Of travelling?'

Martha turned her head to look straight at him. 'Of not having any commitments to go home to,' she said.

There was a pause. Lewis found himself staring back at her as if riveted by the brown eyes, until he managed to wrench his gaze away.

'I decided a long time ago that I wasn't getting involved with family life,' he said flatly. 'I'm not going to be responsible for putting any more children through what Savannah and I went through.'

'You know, it doesn't have to be that way,' she said quietly. 'Not all mothers walk out on their children.'

'Maybe not, but in my experience it doesn't take them long to get bored, no matter what they say about the joys of being a mother.' Lewis's expression was hard. 'Did I tell you that I had an email from Helen yesterday?'

Helen. The beautiful girlfriend. The one he missed.

Martha stiffened in spite of herself. 'Oh?'

'She told me she'd had a baby girl, and was ecstatically happy.'

Was he jealous? 'Oh. Well…that's good.'

'Helen's gone back to work already, but she tells me that the nanny is wonderful,' Lewis went on abrasively. 'Apparently I've got no idea how fantastic family life can be.'

'I don't know about that,' said Martha. 'Here you are, sitting over Sunday lunch, with two babies sleeping under a tree. Isn't that what family life is all about?'

Lewis glanced over towards Viola and Noah, sleeping soundly the way only babies could.

'We're not a family,' he said.

'Not officially, but we're two adults and two children,

and we're living together. We count as a temporary family, don't we?'

'But that's the thing about families,' he objected. 'They're not temporary. Families should stay together, shouldn't they?'

Martha's smile evaporated as she thought about Noah and what she wanted for him. Lewis was right. Temporary wasn't good enough.

'Yes,' she said, 'they should.'

'Have you got any plans for today?' Lewis asked one morning later the following week as he swallowed the last of his coffee.

'Just the usual,' said Martha, wiping Viola's face and hands. 'Why?'

'I thought you might like to come into town and I'll take you out to lunch. Eloise will keep an eye on these two, won't she?'

'I'm sure she will.' Martha concentrated on not looking too excited. It was only lunch after all. And it was only Lewis. Not exactly a hot date, then. And no reason for her heart to start skittering around in her chest.

'About twelve-thirty, then?'

'Sure. Fine. Thanks.'

She couldn't wait for him to go so that she could start smiling.

'And don't look at me like that,' she told Noah and Viola, who were staring at her with identically sceptical expressions. 'I'm allowed to go out to lunch, aren't I? I'm not going to do anything stupid.'

Like fall for a man who had made it crystal-clear that he wasn't going to be part of any family. Martha sobered at the thought. It would be too easy to forget, but a family was what Noah needed. Lewis hadn't said anything more about asking around about Rory, and she hadn't liked to nag him about it.

Hadn't thought about it at all, she corrected herself guiltily.

She really should make more of an effort. The days were slipping by, and she hadn't even *tried* to find Rory herself. It was hard to believe now that she had spent all those months in London fixated on the idea of getting out here so that she could introduce Noah to his father. Somehow it didn't seem quite so important now, and Martha felt ashamed of herself. Rory was Noah's father. He was the reason she was here, and it was still important to find him.

Maybe Lewis would introduce her to some people today. She could ask if anyone knew Rory. That was a better reason for wanting to go to lunch than the thought of sitting next to Lewis and hearing his voice and watching the way his eyes creased when he smiled.

She had agreed to meet him at a restaurant in Perpetua's one and only main street. Martha's plan was to get there early and to be waiting serenely when Lewis arrived but, as so often in life, things didn't quite turn out the way she had imagined them. First Noah needed his nappy changed, and then Viola threw a tantrum which meant that Martha forgot to take her umbrella, which was just asking for the heavens to open, which they duly did, waiting until she just about halfway so she was going to get drenched whichever way she ran.

So serene was the last thing Martha was feeling as she squelched up the restaurant steps nearly twenty minutes late. She paused in the doorway, wiping the rain from her face with the back of her hands, and making a futile attempt to wring the worst of the water from her dress.

She had deliberately chosen a pretty one that Lewis hadn't seen before. She had bought it years earlier, when boho chic was all the rage and, although it was old and faded now, it was still one of her favourites. The soft colours and floaty material always made her feel very feminine.

The effect wasn't the same when it was wet. Glancing down at herself, Martha was aghast to realise that the material was practically transparent. Thank God she had worn a bra!

Grimacing, she looked up with a twist of material still between her hands, and spotted Lewis sitting on the far side of the restaurant. He was with a woman about Martha's own age, and she forgot about her dress for a moment as her eyes narrowed. The tables in between them were full, and she couldn't see much beyond the fact that the other woman was very elegant and very blonde. Very attractive, too, if ice maidens were your thing, Martha supposed sourly.

And it looked as if they might be Lewis's. He wasn't exactly fawning over the woman—this was Lewis Mansfield, after all, and fawning was not his style—but he was sitting forward and listening, nodding occasionally, and his body language said that he was definitely interested.

Martha's heart sank. Had he used lunch with her as an excuse to invite the other woman along, or had he joined her when it looked as if Martha wasn't coming? Either way, it didn't look as if he needed her now. Perhaps she should just slip away?

But she had hesitated too long. Lewis glanced across the room and saw her lurking in the doorway, and for a fleeting instant his face blazed with an expression that was so quickly veiled by his normal, slightly exasperated look that Martha had no chance to interpret it and decided in the end that she must have imagined it. He was beckoning her irritably now. Too late to make her escape.

Martha made her way across the restaurant, leaving a

trail of wet footprints on the wooden floor. Her dress was clinging to her, clammy and uncomfortable, and her hair was hanging in rats' tails. She didn't feel pretty and feminine now. She felt like a moron.

Lewis got to his feet as she reached the table. 'Where on earth have you been?' he said by way of a greeting. 'I was beginning to think something had happened to you.'

'Something did happen to me—your niece! I was late by the time I'd sorted her out, and then I was rushing, and of course I forgot my umbrella…'

'So I see.' Lewis's derisive gaze rested on her for a quelling moment before he pulled out a chair between him and the ice maiden. Martha was depressed to note that close up she looked even crisper and more elegant than she had from a distance.

'You'd better sit down,' he said. 'That dress isn't decent.'

He made the introductions. The ice maiden was called Candace Stephens. 'Candace is manager of a new resort that's just been opened along the coast from here,' he told Martha.

'We're hoping to take advantage of the new airport.' Candace smiled prettily, but Martha wasn't fooled. Candace was interested in more than the length of Lewis's runways. She could see it in her eyes.

'Martha is Viola's nanny,' Lewis finished the introductions.

Oh, that was great! How to make her feel completely insignificant in one easy move! Viola's nanny…was that really all she was?

'And cook,' said Martha defiantly. 'Don't forget that.'

'It must be marvellous to have a job where you use your hands,' sighed Candace. 'So much more relaxing than spending all day in boring meetings—oh, I don't mean with *you*!' She laughed across the table at Lewis and put out her hand towards him, although he hadn't fed her any cue and, indeed, had his distant look on.

Martha eyed Candace with dislike. Why not come right out and accuse her of having a mindless job while they were having high-powered meetings about how many jumbo jet-loads of tourists could land at his precious airport?

'Well, it's a nice idea,' she said frostily, 'but you don't get much chance to relax when you're looking after two babies.'

'Two?' Candace lifted perfectly shaped eyebrows, the kind of brows Martha used to have in the days when she had had time to go to a beautician. 'I thought you just had your niece with you?' she said to Lewis.

Oh, so she and Lewis had been exchanging life stories, had they? Martha wiped a trickle of water from her neck and opened the menu with a snap. She didn't know what was worse, that he had told her about Viola, or that he hadn't mentioned Noah.

'Noah is Martha's son,' said Lewis. 'He's the same age as Viola, so they do everything together.'

He was trying not to look at Martha, but it was difficult when she was sitting there with that damned dress clinging to her and her eyes snapping dangerously. Her lashes were spiky with rain, her hair still plastered to her head, and a drop of water was trickling tantalisingly from her clavicle down towards her cleavage. Lewis wanted to reach out and stop it with his finger, to stop her looking disturbingly sexy. He didn't like the way the other men in the restaurant had followed her with their eyes as she walked across the room.

He wished he hadn't invited her to lunch now. Seeing her on her own like this made it harder to think of her as just Viola's nanny, just an employee. But he'd promised to introduce her to some people, and he'd thought that she and Candace would get on.

Big mistake. They both had that tight-jawed look of people forced to be polite and hating every second of it.

'Oh, you've got a baby?' Candace was saying with an unnecessarily baffled air, as if Noah were a giraffe, or a pet slug.

'That's right,' said Martha tersely, without lifting her eyes from the menu. 'I'm a single mother.'

'How brave of you!'

Martha looked up at that. 'Why do you say that?' she asked with a challenging stare.

'Well, it's a lot to take on, isn't it?' The pitying note in Candace's voice set Martha's teeth on edge. 'It's exhausting enough when you can share the child care with a partner. I can't tell you how many friends I've seen go from bright, go-ahead women to brain-dead zombies who can't talk about anything except breast pumps and sleeping patterns! They all had really promising careers, but they've given it all up—and for what? The torture of no sleep and no stimulation!'

Candace gave an exaggerated shudder. 'It's not for me.'

'No, it doesn't sound as if you would be a very good mother,' said Martha evenly. 'You should have lots in common with Lewis, though. He's not keen on procreating either, are you?'

Lewis frowned but Candace's eyes narrowed with renewed interest. After that, there was no stopping her. She manoeuvred the conversation to business, and kept it firmly there.

Martha wondered what she was supposed to contribute. A bright account of how many nappies she had changed yesterday, perhaps, or a description of Viola's runny nose?

As it was, she ate her lunch and observed Candace's technique sourly. She could practically see the other woman's mind working furiously. There wouldn't be that many eligible men on an island this size, and Martha could just imagine how Candace's eyes must have lit up when Lewis swam into view.

She had probably been disappointed when she discovered that they weren't lunching alone, and it may have seemed on paper as if Viola's nanny, actually sharing a house with him, would be a bit of a threat, but one look at Martha in her bedraggled state must have reassured her. And, of course, knowing that he had no interest in babies either would mean that they had one more thing in common.

Surely, Candace was no doubt thinking, Lewis would be looking for a woman who was as dedicated to her career as he was. That would explain why she was rabbiting on about it, Martha thought, profoundly unimpressed. Candace was only managing a hotel, for God's sake. It didn't take a genius to organise a rota for receptionists or make sure the chambermaids changed the towels, did it? Anyone would think Candace was finding a cure for cancer the way she was carrying on.

It was difficult to tell what Lewis thought of her. Martha studied him from under her lashes. He responded politely enough, and she had to admit that he made an effort to include her in the conversation, but Candace wasn't having any of it. She was bent on pointing up the contrast between her own blonde elegance and efficiency and Martha, left wet and crumpled and with nothing to talk about.

It would have been amusing if Candace hadn't been quite so pretty, Martha thought glumly. She was tall and statuesque, with perfect skin and green eyes, and her platinum blonde hair was drawn back from her face in a neat French twist. She would have been beautiful if she had more warmth and animation.

But maybe Lewis didn't care about that. He was hardly

the king of warm and caring himself, was he? Martha sighed as she put down her fork, thinking of how much she had looked forward to her lunch. She should have known. If they could have spoken, even Noah and Viola could probably have told her that it would turn out like this.

She had been living in a dangerous dream world where the fact that Lewis didn't want children and didn't want to be part of a family and wouldn't want her even if he did was conveniently forgotten. Time to wake up and smell the coffee, as they had said at *Glitz*.

'I'd better get back,' she said as soon as she had finished eating. 'It's not fair to leave Eloise too long with the twins. Don't get up,' she added as Lewis made to push back his chair. 'You two stay and finish your meal.'

Lewis looked as if he were about to protest but Candace was smiling prettily. 'I'd love a coffee,' she said, apparently deciding that the leisure industry could survive a few more minutes without her.

'I'll see you later,' Martha said coolly to Lewis. 'Thanks for lunch.'

'You're very quiet,' Lewis said later that night, when the babies were in bed and Martha was serving up supper.

'You know me,' said Martha, banging saucepans around. 'Nothing to talk about except breast pumps and sleeping patterns! I don't want to bore you.'

The odd thing was that he had never felt bored when he was with Martha. Why was that? Lewis wondered, distracted for a moment, but she was obviously in a bad mood and it wasn't hard to guess the reason why.

Sighing, he moved out of her way as she reached for a salad bowl. 'Look, I'm sorry about lunch,' he said. 'I only invited Candace because you said you wanted to meet some new people. I thought you would get on.'

'Really?' said Martha tightly, tearing up lettuce with a kind of savagery. 'What on earth made you think that?'

Lewis shrugged. 'You're both the same sort of age, both single women, both expats…'

'Oh, and that's supposed to make us friends, is it? Forget the fact that we have absolutely nothing else in common!'

'I didn't realise that when I invited her to lunch,' he said, holding on to his temper with difficulty. 'I met her at some meeting and she said she'd just arrived on the island and hadn't had a chance to make many friends. I hardly know her.'

'You surprise me.' Martha took a knife to some tomatoes. 'She seemed to think that she knew *you*. No prizes for guessing whose friend Candace wants to be!'

He looked wary. 'What do you mean?'

'Come on, Lewis, it's obvious she's interested in you! I've never felt such a gooseberry. She didn't want me there, spoiling things and being downtrodden and boring and oppressed by motherhood!'

Lewis sucked in an irritable breath. 'I've told you, I barely know Candace.'

'Well, that can change. You should go for it,' said Martha with a brittle smile as she scraped the tomatoes into the bowl. To hell with presentation. 'Candace's perfect for you. You know she's not going to do a Helen and go all broody on you, so you can have a lovely time comparing your high-powered careers and pitying poor schmucks like me who tie themselves down with children and think happiness and love and security are more important than promotion or winning some contract!'

Lewis's mouth tightened. He didn't understand why she was so cross. So lunch hadn't been a success. It wasn't his fault they hadn't got on, was it? At least he had made an effort to introduce her. There was no need for all this fuss. If anything, she should have been grateful.

He scowled as Martha put the salad on the dining table. He didn't like it when women were irrational like this. He didn't like their baffling leaps of logic. But mostly he didn't like the way he hadn't been able to stop thinking about her in that wet dress.

He had hardly got any work done that afternoon. It was pathetic. Pathetic how disappointed he had been to come home and find her back in loose trousers and a sleeveless shirt, looking cool and chic and utterly different from the way she had looked in the restaurant, all hot and bothered and dripping, with the sodden dress clinging to her skin so that he could see her warm curves—

'What?' He jerked back to attention.

'I said, are you coming to sit down?'

'Yes.' Lewis cleared his throat. 'Yes, of course.'

Viola was fretful all evening and Martha had to get up from the table to her a couple of times. 'I think she might be getting a cold,' she said, feeling the hot little forehead. 'If she's not better in the morning I'll find a doctor.'

In the meantime, there was a whole night to get through. Martha dosed the baby up with what she had, but Viola refused to settle. She would wake up crying, allow herself to be comforted and go back to sleep, only to start again a few minutes later.

Eventually, she woke Noah, who started to grizzle. Martha had Viola in one arm, and was leaning over Noah's cot, trying to comfort him with her other hand, when Lewis appeared.

'It sounds like you need a hand,' he said.

Martha was too tired by then to stand on ceremony. She had no idea what time it was, and her ears were ringing with the combined sound of two crying babies. 'Do you think you could walk Noah round for a bit while I give Viola some water?'

She made up a bottle in the kitchen one-handed, and took it back into the living area to collapse onto the sofa. Cradling Viola in her arms, she offered her the drink and, to her relief, it seemed to be what the baby wanted. She stopped crying, and for a while there was a blissful silence. Martha let her head fall back against the cushions in weary relief.

Lewis was pacing up and down in front of the sliding doors that led out on to the verandah. He was wearing the same loose grey pyjama bottoms that he had worn before, and was holding Noah against his bare chest. Martha watched him languorously from under drooping lashes. He was rubbing the baby's back, the big hands circling in a gentle rhythm, while Noah cuddled into his neck and sucked his thumb, a sure sign that he was comforted.

Lucky Noah. The thought popped treacherously into Martha's head and she straightened abruptly and turned her attention back to Viola.

'How's she doing?' Lewis asked softly.

'Fine.' Martha's voice sounded horribly brittle. 'I think she may sleep after this. I hope so, anyway.'

'This little chap's almost asleep too.'

To her horror, he came to sit next to her on the sofa, and every single one of Martha's senses jerked and jangled with a disturbing awareness. Stretching out his legs in front of him, Lewis let out a long, weary breath. 'It would be nice to get some sleep tonight,' he said.

'Yes,' said Martha huskily, her eyes riveted on his feet because that seemed safer than staring at the rest of him, but even they were distracting. Nice toes, she found herself thinking. Nice everything.

He was so close. Not awkwardly so, but definitely close

enough to touch if she wanted to. Which she didn't. Shouldn't, anyway.

But her fingers still itched to reach out and feel the solid warmth of his body. That would be a bad idea, Martha reminded herself. A very bad idea, because…because… She sought frantically for a reason why it would be so bad.

Because of her responsibility to Noah. She seized on the thought. That was right. Noah needed a father, so there was no point in getting involved with a man who didn't want children, didn't want a family, a man with whom she and her son could never share a future.

It wasn't even as if Lewis were that attractive, she told herself with an edge of desperation. His nose was too big, his brows too fierce, his jaw too strong. He was dour and deliberate and infuriatingly logical. He was stern and stubborn, reserved and probably repressed. There was no reason to find him attractive.

No reason to want to touch him, to know whether his mouth was as cool and firm as it looked. No reason to want the feel of his hands on her body. No reason to think about burrowing into him and pressing her lips to his throat and tasting his skin.

No reason at all. Martha drew a shuddering breath and Lewis turned his head to look at her closely.

'You must be tired,' he said.

'Yes…yes, I am tired,' she said huskily

That must be all it was. It was dark and late and the tropical night was heady with perfume and the rasp of insects and the seductive murmur of the ocean beyond the palms, and she was just tired. That was why her heart was thumping in time with the ceiling fan overhead. That was why her blood was beating and booming beneath her skin, and her mind was fuzzy with desire, and her bones had dissolved.

Tiredness. That was all it was.

'Let me see if he'll go down.' Lewis levered himself up and took Noah into the bedroom. Half relieved, half disappointed, Martha remembered Viola and looked down to see her ridiculously long lashes fluttering and the teat of the bottle slipping from her mouth. She was asleep too.

'I'll take her.' Lewis was back. Reaching down, he lifted his niece gently from Martha's arms, and the brush of his hands against her bare skin was enough to make her heart clench with desire.

She should get up and go to bed. Martha knew that, but she couldn't move. She felt boneless and giddy. *I'm just tired*, she said to herself like a mantra. Just tired. *That's all.*

CHAPTER SEVEN

'COME on, time for bed.' Lewis spoke above her, and Martha opened her eyes, huge and dark in the dim light. There was something odd about his voice, but she couldn't pinpoint what it was.

'I'm too tired to move,' she managed. 'I think I'll stay here.'

'You'd be better off in bed.' Lewis held down a hand. 'Here, I'll help you up.'

Martha stared at his hand. She had the oddest feeling that her whole life had come down to this moment, that she had reached the point where her future forked. Taking his hand would lead one way, refusing it another.

She shook her head slightly. This was silly. She was so tired she wasn't thinking straight. Lewis wasn't offering her a life-changing choice. He was offering her a hand to help her upright.

She smiled wearily up at him. 'Sorry, I'm just a bit dopey,' she said, and took his hand.

As soon as she felt his fingers close firmly around hers, Martha knew that she had made a mistake. He drew her up, but it was as if all her bones had liquefied, so that she had to cling to his hand as the only thing holding her upright. Her legs gave way and she would have fallen if Lewis hadn't felt her buckle and clamped her instinctively to him.

Martha gasped at the feel of his body, just as hard and solid as she had imagined. His bare shoulder was only millimetres from her mouth, his skin a breath away from her own. With one detached part of her mind she knew that it should be possible to avoid Lewis's gaze and step past him with a polite apology, but somehow she couldn't do it. Something a lot stronger and more insistent made her lift her eyes instead and look straight into Lewis's face, and what she read there made the breath leak from her lungs.

There was a long, long moment when time seemed to stretch into infinity as they stared at each other. Afterwards, Martha was never sure what had shattered that breathless pause. Did she kiss Lewis, or did he kiss her? It didn't matter, anyway. All that mattered was that in a burst of glorious release from the tension they were kissing, deep, hot, hungry kisses, and it felt wonderful.

Gasping, still kissing, they sank back down on to the sofa, and she wrapped her arms around him, craving the feel of his body, so hard, so sure against hers. Dizzy with the relief of being able to touch him at last, she ran her hands over his bare back, down his flanks, up over his shoulders, revelling in the feel of him, and all the time his mouth was demanding, his hands insistent, exploring, under her knees, over her thighs, easing beneath her shirt until she shuddered and arched towards him.

God, it felt so good! Martha couldn't remember how she had been able to convince herself that it would be a bad idea. It was a great idea. A *fantastic* idea. How could anything that felt this exciting and right not be?

She wound her arms around him and kissed Lewis back as he rolled her beneath him, tipping her head back to let him press kisses down the side of her neck in a way that made her shiver deliciously. Her head was spinning with sheer sensation, and there was nothing but the feel of his body and the touch of his lips and their ragged breathing...

...and dimly, distantly, the sound of a baby crying.

Lewis heard it at the same time and he stilled, dropping his forehead on to her shoulder for a moment before he lifted his head reluctantly and looked down into Martha's face.

She never forgot the way his expression cleared with shock. 'God, what am I doing?' he said blankly.

Martha had never been with a man who had kissed her the way Lewis had, or made her feel the way he had, but she had certainly had kisses that ended with more finesse. As a way of letting her know that he hadn't meant to kiss her at all, and was horrified to realise that he had, it could hardly be bettered. Anyone would think he had picked up a slug in the dark.

Mortified, Martha struggled upright. 'That's Viola,' she managed shakily. 'I'd better go.'

Lewis put his head in his hands with a muttered expletive as she tugged down her shirt, ignoring the fact that it was too late for modesty, and somehow made it on trembling legs to Viola's cot. A few gentle pats and a murmured word were all it took to reassure the baby, who was soon asleep again.

Martha lingered by the cot, envying Viola her ability to relax completely. If only a few pats were enough to comfort *her*! Not that there were likely to be many pats coming her way in the near future. Judging by Lewis's expression as he levered himself off her, he would never touch her again.

Martha's throat closed painfully at the thought. Was it her fault? Had she just grabbed him? she wondered desperately. Oh, God, what if she had? What if he had just been too polite to push her away? A deep flush spread through her as she remembered how wonderful it had felt to kiss him, how eagerly she had responded. She had been all over Lewis, kissing him, touching him. No wonder he had been horrified!

Martha looked down at the sleeping babies and wished she could be sound asleep too. Maybe then she would wake up and find that she hadn't made a complete fool of herself in front of Lewis after all. But her body was still twitching and tingling, and her lips were swollen, and the memories were much, much too vivid to have been a dream.

Which meant that some time she was going to have to stop lurking in here and face him again. And say what? Sorry, Lewis, just got a bit carried away by my hormones there? Was it too late to blame it on jet lag? Except feeling jet lagged didn't normally involve dragging your employer on to a sofa and ravishing him.

Sighing, Martha ran her fingers through her hair in despair.

'Is Viola all right?'

Lewis's voice in the doorway made her heart jerk so violently it was a moment before she could speak.

'She's fine,' she muttered.

He hesitated. 'Are you OK?'

'I'm fine,' said Martha, still without looking at him.

Another pause, and then Lewis turned on his heel. 'I'll leave you to it, then,' he said curtly. A moment later Martha heard the sound of his bedroom door being very firmly closed. He was probably wedging a chair under the handle in case she tried to follow him.

So, that was one problem solved. If Lewis was going to pretend that nothing had happened she would be spared the need to come up with a convincing explanation as to why she had jumped him like that.

Martha was torn between relief and a gathering fury. How dared he pretend nothing had happened? Something most definitely had happened! And, OK, it might have been her that started it, but it took two, and he had been joining in there. If Viola hadn't cried...

Just thinking about what would have happened if Viola hadn't woken up right then made Martha want to bang on

Lewis's bedroom door and demand that he finish what he had started. It wasn't fair to set her on fire like that and then decide to *leave her to it*.

It was probably better, though. Martha blew out a long sigh. Lewis was right. The situation was awkward for both of them, but they were grown-ups, so they would just have to deal with it. And the best way to do that was to ignore the fact that they had kissed at all, forget the thrill of his hands and his lips on her body, pretend that she didn't know how it felt to be pressed beneath that hard body, that she couldn't imagine the rocketing excitement, that she had never arched to his touch. That she hadn't wanted it to stop.

If Lewis could do all that, then so could she.

She could try, anyway.

'I owe you an apology.'

Lewis put his mug down on the counter and looked straight at Martha. They had exchanged strained greetings when she carried Noah into the kitchen early the next day. After her active night, Viola was still sleeping peacefully, and Martha concentrated fiercely on putting Noah in his high chair, finding him a drink, anything other than face the taut silence.

She had hardly slept, and her body was buzzing and thumping in a peculiar combination of exhaustion and frustration. Her only consolation had been the certainty that Lewis wouldn't say anything so that she could pretend that nothing had ever happened at all, and now here he was, raising the subject before she was in any state to discuss anything, let alone that. She wasn't even dressed, and it didn't help that Lewis now knew for sure exactly how little she wore underneath her old shirt.

'There's no need for you to apologise,' she said almost crossly.

'I think there is.'

Lewis set his jaw. He wished she wasn't wearing that shirt. It reminded him too vividly of the night before, when she had been sitting in the half-light, and as she had cradled the baby in her arms one sleeve had slipped slightly off her shoulder to reveal the seductive line of her clavicle. Her hair had been mussed and her eyes dark. She had looked tired and tousled and sexy, and he hadn't been able to keep his eyes off her, or stop thinking about what it would be like to touch her.

He hadn't meant to kiss her. He had thought that he had himself well under control, thought that he had taken on board all the reasons why touching her would be a really bad idea. When he had held down his hand to help her up he had really believed that the best thing would be if they went to their very separate beds.

But then she had fallen against him and he had felt how soft she was, and how warm, and his mind had gone blank, and the next thing he had known they were on the sofa and all his stern resolutions had evaporated in the excitement that rocketed so unexpectedly and so unstoppably. Only a saint would have remembered that he wasn't supposed to kiss her at all.

'I should never have touched you last night,' he said, squaring his shoulders. 'I didn't mean to, and I'm still not quite sure how it happened, but that's no excuse. It was unacceptable to grab you like that and…'

He trailed off into a sizzling pause while they both remembered what had come next.

'Anyway,' said Lewis, regrouping with an effort, 'I'm sorry. You're my employee and you'd be well within your rights to object to the way I behaved last night. I'm paying you to look after Viola, not to…to…' He was getting on to dangerous ground again. He had a nasty feeling he was making things worse, not better. Maybe it would be better not to finish that sentence?

'You should feel safe,' he said instead, 'and not as if you're going to be harassed like that at any time.'

Martha eyed him a little uncertainly. The disjointed apology had banished her crossness with him for raising the matter at all far more effectively than a fluent one would have done. Lewis was a proud man and it must have cost him a lot, she realised. And it really wasn't fair for him to take all of the blame on himself.

'I wouldn't call it harassment,' she said carefully. 'It was just…one of those things. We were both tired, and I think we both got a bit carried away. I don't think either of us really knew what we were doing.'

Lewis was a little daunted by her coolness. *Just one of those things?* She made it sound as if she got kissed on sofas like that all the time. He shook himself mentally. He ought to be grateful that Martha was taking the whole business in her stride, and not storming off back to London or ringing up her solicitor to press charges.

'It's kind of you to look at it that way,' he said formally. No harm in showing her that he could be cool, too. 'But it doesn't change the fact that I'm sorry. I really just wanted to reassure you that it won't happen again.'

Somehow, that wasn't quite what Martha wanted to hear, but she could hardly tell him that.

'I think it would be best if we both forgot all about it,' she said instead.

'Right,' said Lewis. 'Right. Yes. Let's do that.'

Of course, forget it. Why hadn't he suggested that? It should be easy enough. He had plenty of other things to think about. There were the preliminary surveys to be organised, meetings to be had, reports to write, analyses to do. They had run into a legal problem about acquiring land for the airport extension, and there was a looming problem

with one of the contracts… No, the last thing he had time
to do was brood over a little kiss. He had much more
important things on his mind.

And yet, it was funny how hard it was to shift the memory of the heat of her mouth and the softness of her skin
and all the warm, vital, responsive warmth of her. As the
days passed, Lewis found himself increasingly unsettled.
Those memories had an alarming ability to sneak into his
mind at odd moments, when he was supposed to be fo-
cusing on something else entirely, on something *important*.

Disquieted by his apparent inability to shrug them off,
he became even more brusque than usual. The office manager and PA took to treading warily around him at work,
and at home things were even worse. In spite—or perhaps
because—of the efforts he and Martha made to carry on
as normal, the atmosphere between them was horribly con-
strained.

Everywhere reminded him of Martha. The living room,
where the sofa practically pulsated with memories. The
verandah, where in easier times they used to sit in the dark
and listen to the sea. They never did that any more, and
Lewis missed it more than he wanted to admit. The
kitchen, where every morning Martha gave the babies their
breakfast barefoot, wearing nothing but that damned shirt,
and his fingers itched to catch at it and pull her closer, to
tell her it wasn't working, that he couldn't forget.

He wouldn't do it, of course. That would just be asking
for trouble, Lewis knew that. Martha was Viola's nanny.
Why did he have to keep reminding himself of that fact?
What was more, she was good at her job. Even to Lewis's
inexperienced eye it was obvious how loving and gentle
but firm she was with both babies, and she treated Viola
as if she really was Noah's twin.

So he didn't want to lose her as his employee, did he?
She was a good cook too. It would be stupid to jeopardise

a successful business relationship just because the memory of how warm and responsive she had been kept snagging at his attention.

Very stupid.

And anyway, Martha wasn't really his type, Lewis tried to rationalise it when the employee argument seemed less persuasive. He had always preferred cool, independent women. It made him nervous when they got clingy and needy and started talking about commitment.

Martha hadn't done that yet, but it was obvious what she wanted. She already had a baby and she was looking for a family, with all the mess and complications and emotions that involved. Lewis didn't want any of that, and it would be unfair to pretend that he did, just to get her into bed and satisfy what was clearly only a temporary obsession.

In any case, she had never given the slightest sign that she would want him, Lewis reminded himself. Apart from that night on the sofa, of course, and as she had said that had just been a case of getting a bit carried away. She had been very clear right from the start that her priority was to find Noah's father. Lewis wasn't about to volunteer for that role, not with his experience of family life.

What he needed, Lewis decided, was a distraction. Bumping into Candace Stephens outside the office one day gave him the perfect opportunity, and he invited her out to lunch straight away, almost as if he needed to prove something. Although he wasn't quite sure whether he was proving it to Martha or to himself.

Candace was much more suitable, Lewis told himself, observing her approvingly over lunch. She was cool and rational and very attractive, and she was insistent about the fact that her career came first. Candace had no time for messy babies or messy emotions. She had her own life, her own job, her own priorities. She wouldn't want to get too involved with anyone. She was perfect for him, in fact.

So what if his skin didn't tingle when he caught sight of her? It didn't matter that Candace didn't have a lush mouth that made his mind go hazy. Lewis told himself that it was a good thing that he could talk to her without being distracted by the sheen of her skin or the silkiness of her hair. Candace was just the distraction he needed.

'I won't be in for supper tomorrow night.' He broke the silence over the meal the next day.

Martha had been toying listlessly with her salad, but she looked up at that. 'Oh?'

'There's some function at the hotel where Candace Stephens is manager.' For some reason Lewis found himself stumbling a little over his explanation. 'She asked if I would like to go along, and I thought—'

Why didn't he just say that he was going out with Candace? Martha wondered crossly. 'You don't need to explain to me,' she interrupted him. 'What you do with your private life is your own business. But thank you for letting me know,' she added with quelling politeness.

Lewis hesitated. 'Will you be all right here on your own all evening?'

'Of course,' she said with a brittle smile. 'I'm quite used to it.'

Which wasn't *quite* true any more. She was used to Lewis being there now. Used to the involuntary jerk of her senses whenever he walked into the room. Used to the way her heart missed a beat at the thought of him.

She was even getting used to lying awake at night and reliving that kiss as it played in an endless loop in her head. And she was learning to accept that when Lewis had said that it wouldn't happen again he had meant it.

Now it looked as if she was going to have to accept that

he was going out with Candace, too. That would be nearly as hard, but she could do it. She didn't need Lewis.

'I'm sure Eloise would come over if you wanted.'

Great. Not only was Lewis appalled at the thought of kissing her, he thought she was too pathetic to spend a few hours in a house on her own. What kind of drip did he think she was?

Martha surveyed him coolly. 'You know, I've held down a demanding job and I look after two babies all day, which is even more demanding. I think I can survive an evening on my own! Viola and Noah may need a baby-sitter, but at thirty-four I think I'm a bit old for one, don't you?'

Lewis scowled. He didn't like it when she was sarcastic. 'I was only trying to think of you,' he said grouchily.

If he were really thinking of her, he wouldn't be going out with Candace, would he? Martha put up her chin.

'You can think of me by asking around at this function tomorrow night and seeing if anyone has heard of Rory,' she told him crisply.

Rory. The toyboy she was so obsessed about. Lewis had almost let himself forget about Rory, and the blunt reminder made the intimidating brows draw together. 'Haven't you found him yet?'

'When do I have a chance to look for him?' countered Martha. 'I'm stuck here all the time!'

'I thought you went out every day?'

'Only to the market, and my Creole's not up to interrogating stallholders yet!'

There were probably lots of other things that she could have done, especially with Eloise to help, but Martha didn't feel like admitting to Lewis that so far she hadn't made any effort at all to find Noah's father. It wasn't that she didn't think about him, she did. Occasionally, anyway, when she looked at Noah. The truth, though, was that recently she had spent a lot more time thinking about Lewis and how he had kissed her than she had about Rory.

Not that she had any intention of admitting *that* to Lewis either!

'I introduced you to Candace,' Lewis pointed out. 'If you had really wanted to get out more you could have followed that acquaintance up.'

'Funnily enough, I didn't see us becoming bosom buddies, her being such a clever career woman and me being a brain-dead zombie with nothing better to do than look after two children!'

'You didn't need to be close friends for her to introduce you to some other people,' said Lewis, pointedly not denying that she was a brain-dead zombie, which Martha thought wouldn't have cost him anything.

'Well, it's not that I didn't appreciate the thought,' she said tartly, 'but maybe next time you could introduce me to someone a little less chilly, and I might make more of an effort.'

Chilly. Lewis couldn't shake the word whenever he looked at Candace the next evening. She was stunning in a silvery sheath dress, but there was something off-putting about her cool beauty. He couldn't help comparing her to Martha, with her dark eyes and her hot mouth and her warm smile, the opposite of chilly.

He didn't like socialising at the best of times, and the evening seemed interminable. Candace was very much on duty, and he was left to make small talk and watch the door, almost as if he were hoping that Martha might miraculously walk in, which was a ridiculous thing to do.

Making his excuses to Candace, he left as early as he could, but Martha had gone to bed anyway by the time he got home. Lewis was furious with himself for being disappointed. He sat on the verandah and scowled at the tropical night and told himself that he was a fool.

Martha was determinedly bright the next morning. 'Did you have a nice time?' she asked, even though Lewis was obviously in a foul mood.

He shrugged. 'It was just one of those parties where you stand around and talk to a load of people you don't know and don't particularly want to.'

'Remind me not to invite you to any of my parties!' said Martha, eyeing him curiously. 'You must have met someone interesting—apart from Candace, of course,' she added snidely. 'I can see how interesting she would be to you!'

Lewis glared at her. 'I didn't meet anyone who knows Rory, if that's what you want to know,' he snapped.

Martha was momentarily taken aback. She had forgotten that she had asked him to see if anyone knew Rory but, now that he had mentioned it, it was an excellent reason for her to be so interested in the party. Nothing to do with wanting to know how he had got on with Candace, for instance.

'Someone must know him,' she said, changing tack. 'It's such a tiny place.'

'Well, if they do they'll be at the reception at the High Commission next week,' said Lewis. 'I accepted an invitation for you, so you can ask around yourself.'

'An invitation?' Startled, Martha paused in the middle of wiping Viola's face and hands. 'For me?'

'They usually invite all the Brits in a place like this.' Lewis drank his coffee, embarrassed to remember that talking about her, even mentioning her name, had been about his only pleasure the night before. 'I told the High Commissioner that you were grumbling about never going anywhere or meeting anyone, and she said we would both get an invitation to the reception. If you don't meet anyone who knows Rory there, you've got the wrong island.'

'Oh.' Martha heard the doubt in her own voice and

caught herself up. She ought to be sounding a lot more enthusiastic than that. 'Well...thank you,' she said awkwardly.

What was wrong with her? She ought to be pleased that he had gone to so much effort. Thanks to Lewis, she was a step closer to finding Rory, and she should be grateful, not wondering whether his concern to increase her social life was part of a more complex strategy to get her out of the way.

Perhaps he was really keen on Candace, after all, and afraid that she would hang around casting darkling glances at the sofa and cramping his style? Martha cringed at the very thought. She would just have to show him that, as far as she was concerned, he could do whatever he liked. If it seemed a pity that he should choose a block of ice like Candace Stephens, well, that was none of her business. His mouth was more than capable of melting ice in any case...

Her thoughts were wandering dangerously. Martha pulled herself together. Lewis had made an effort for her, so she could do the same for him. And she could start by being a lot nicer about Candace, otherwise he might suspect that she was jealous of the other woman.

Which was nonsense, of course.

'If you want to return Candace's invitation by having her to dinner here, I'd be happy to cook for you,' she said, lifting first Noah then Viola out of their high chairs and setting them on the floor, where they liked to bang wooden spoons against a saucepan. As entertainment it was cheap and effective, if a bit noisy at times.

'I could make something nice,' she persevered when Lewis didn't respond immediately. 'And you needn't worry about me hanging around. I'd stay in the kitchen.'

'Frankly, I don't think I'd enjoy my meal with the thought of you lurking behind the kitchen door,' said

Lewis acerbically. 'There'd be no question of you not *hanging around*, as you put it.'

He hesitated, reluctant to admit even to himself that he didn't really want to spend an evening alone with Candace.

'I tell you what you could do for me, though,' he said. 'I've got a hydrologist, a botanist and an economist arriving tomorrow, to do the preliminary studies for the World Bank. They're just on short-term contracts, so they'll be staying at a hotel—Candace's hotel, in fact—but it would be nice to offer them some home cooking as a change from eating out in restaurants every night. Perhaps I could invite them to supper next week, and invite Candace at the same time?'

Martha brightened. Just because she liked cooking, she told herself. Nothing to do with the fact that Lewis hadn't jumped at the chance of a *tête à tête* with Candace.

'I'll cook something really nice,' she promised.

She planned her menu carefully and was up early on the day of the dinner party to get to the market when everything was really fresh, and give herself plenty of time to prepare everything. She was determined to produce a spectacular meal, to look stunning and be witty and entertaining, just to prove to Candace that having a baby didn't have to be the equivalent of a lobotomy. Everything was going to be perfect.

And it might have been if Eloise's mother hadn't fallen, if Eloise hadn't had to take her to the hospital. If Martha hadn't had to try and shop and cook and clean the house with the twins in tow at all times. If the fishermen had caught the fish she wanted and there hadn't been an inexplicable absence of her key ingredient in the market. If Viola hadn't been in a particularly contrary mood all day, and especially if Noah hadn't been unusually fretful and chosen to throw up all over the sofa just before she put them to bed.

In the resulting rush to check that he wasn't really ill, and clean up the living room, and settle Viola, who always played up the moment she wasn't the centre of attention, Martha forgot all about her pots on the stove and, by the time she had remembered them, her sauce was curdled, the vegetables disintegrating and her precious pudding that she had been so proud of absolutely ruined.

At least Lewis was able to help her put Noah and Viola to bed when he came home, but Martha was still frantically trying to cobble together an alternative meal when the first guests arrived, and there was no time for her to change and be magically transformed into the relaxed, effortlessly stylish superwoman she had planned.

Wiping her hands on a tea towel, she grimaced as she caught sight of herself in a mirror on her way to be introduced. In her limp T-shirt and the stained trousers she had been wearing all day she looked and felt exactly like the zombie Candace had so patronisingly described. Knowing that the other woman would be delighted to have all her expectations confirmed was the icing on the cake of the day from hell, Martha decided.

'My goodness, you *do* look tired!' exclaimed Candace, glowing and immaculate in a white sheath dress, and Martha had to grit her teeth as Candace ladled on the sympathy until everyone was looking at her in a way that made her acutely conscious of her hair hanging limply, and the fact that she didn't have a scrap of make-up on.

Just what her ego needed.

They were all looking so sorry for her by the time Candace had finished that Martha glanced uneasily down at her herself, suddenly struck with the awful suspicion that she had missed some of Noah's sick on her clothes. She had better steer them all out on to the verandah afterwards and make sure they avoided the sofa.

The botanist and the economist turned out to be young

men who were both very obviously struck by Candace's cool glamour. As an exhausted, rumpled mum, Martha felt completely invisible to them, but she liked the female hydrologist very much, especially when she heard that she was getting married and hoping to have a family of her own.

After the meal, they moved out to the verandah and, while Candace held court talking business strategies with the three men, Martha and Sarah were able to enjoy a cosy chat about babies.

Martha could feel Lewis glance across at them occasionally, but she turned her shoulder defiantly. Let him and Candace roll their eyes about the dullness of her conversation. She didn't care. Noah was her son, and she wasn't ashamed to find him and Viola more interesting than economic analyses, project management, model systems, post-tender evaluations and all the other jargon they were discussing at the other end of the verandah.

She had a good idea that Sarah did, too, in spite of her professionalism. She had heard Martha referring to Viola and Noah as the 'twins' and confided that she was rather worried about the fact that twins ran in her fiancé's family.

'It's not that I mind the idea of having twins,' she told Martha, 'but it does look like a lot of hard work.'

'It's that all right,' said Martha, thinking of the day she had had. 'I don't know how some mothers manage on their own.'

'Yes, you're lucky to have Lewis.' Sarah looked along the verandah to where Lewis was offering around more coffee. 'I haven't worked with him before, but I've heard about the firm, of course. I guess he's so busy that he doesn't get much of a chance to be a real hands-on father?'

'He's not too bad,' Martha began, thinking of the way Lewis came home and helped her put the babies to bed, and then she stopped, belatedly realising what Sarah had said. 'You don't think…? No, Lewis isn't a father at all, and he's no intention of being one either!'

'Oh.' Sarah looked baffled. 'Then you're not his wife?'

'His wife?' Involuntarily, Martha's gaze went to Lewis. He was setting down the coffee pot, smiling in a restrained kind of way, and she felt something unlock inside her. Almost as if he had heard it, he glanced up and their eyes met for a fleeting instant before Martha jerked hers away.

'No,' she said to Sarah, swallowing the tightness in her throat. 'No, I'm not Lewis's wife. I'm sorry, I thought that was obvious.'

Sarah's sharp gaze flicked between Martha and Lewis and she raised her brows. 'No,' she said slowly. 'It's not at all obvious.'

CHAPTER EIGHT

SARAH'S words fell into a lull in the conversation at the other end of the verandah. 'What's not obvious?' asked Candace, so clearly prepared to be amused at what wasn't obvious to two women who had nothing better to do than talk about babies all night that Martha's fingers tightened painfully around the arm of the wicker chair.

'The fact that Lewis and I aren't married,' she said evenly, and turned back to Sarah before she could see Candace smiling smugly at Lewis. 'I'm just the nanny.'

Lewis frowned. 'I'm sorry, Sarah,' he said, scraping back his chair and bringing the coffee pot over to offer them some more. 'I should have introduced Martha properly when you arrived, but we were having a bit of a crisis in the kitchen then.'

Martha couldn't help warming to that 'we', when the crisis had been all hers. Lewis had just been his normal cucumber self, too cool and competent and self-contained to even know what a crisis meant.

'She's helping me look after my niece for a few months,' he was telling Sarah, who was looking completely confused by now.

'We call Viola and Noah the twins because they have the same birthday, but they're not related at all,' Martha explained.

'I see.' Sarah didn't sound as if she did, really. 'So Noah's father...?'

'Is somewhere here on St Bonaventure,' said Martha brightly for Lewis's benefit. 'In fact, I was wondering if you might have heard of him, since you also work in the watery field. He's a marine biologist, not a hydrologist, though. Rory McMillan? I'm keen to get in touch with him while I'm here.'

Sarah shook her head. 'The name doesn't ring a bell with me, I'm afraid, but, of course I've only just arrived. I'll keep an eye out for you, if you like. What does he look like?'

Martha glanced at Lewis. 'Gorgeous,' she said. 'Tall, tanned, blond, dancing blue eyes, fabulous body...you can't miss him!'

Sarah laughed. 'I can see why you're so keen to get in touch with him!'

Candace had given up the pretence of not listening and had turned her chair round to join them, effectively pinning Lewis against the verandah rail where he was leaning and listening to Martha with a scowl.

'I don't recognise the name either,' she said, shamelessly muscling in on the conversation. 'There are quite a lot of marine projects on the outer islands and we sometimes get scientists in the bar or using the pool when they come back to stock up on supplies or pick up the post. I'll ask around for you, Martha, if you like.'

Martha gritted her teeth. She didn't like. It might be perverse not to welcome any offers to help her find Rory, but she could really do without Candace poking her nose into her private business. It was perfectly obvious Candace just wanted to get her out of the way with Rory so that she would have a free run with Lewis—though why the other woman should feel that she was a threat in her grubby T-shirt and trousers stained with sick was a bit of a mystery. As far as sex goddesses went, she wouldn't even make it to the starting line.

'That's kind of you,' she said with what she hoped was quelling civility, 'but there's no need to bother. I'm going to a reception at the High Commission next week, so I'll be able to do any asking around myself then.'

'Oh, you're going to that, are you?'

Martha had to hand it to Candace. The tone was absolutely perfect, subtly implying incredulity that the High Commission should bother to invite a dull, dowdy mother smelling of sick without actually saying anything of the kind.

Sighing inwardly, Martha wondered whether Cinderella had felt like this. Still, there were advantages to the Cinderella role, she consoled herself that night as she lay in bed contemplating the ceiling fan—at least Cinderella got her man and a palace thrown in! Maybe a fairy godmother would materialise on the night of the ball—cheese and wine at the High Commission just didn't have the same ring to it—and fix her up with Prince Charming?

She could do with a Prince Charming right now, Martha thought. Rory was charming enough, good-looking enough, and of course he was Noah's father. Surely she should cast him in the lead role when she tried to imagine her own happy ever after? That was the sensible thing to dream about.

It was just that dreaming would be a lot easier if her mind was in a less contrary mood. She wished it would stop substituting Lewis's austere features for Rory's much more handsome ones. Lewis was all wrong for a hero. He was too dour, too difficult, too determined to avoid family life. Noah needed a father, and if his biological one didn't want the job she would try and find someone else who did. There was no point in wasting time even conjuring up Lewis's face when it came to dreaming about a future.

Unsurprisingly enough, no fairy godmother had appeared by the evening of the reception, but it did seem for once as if the fates were on her side, thought Martha as she got ready to go out. Noah and Viola had been happy all day and had gone to sleep like angels, so she had plenty of time for a shower and to do her hair. Lewis had told her that he would be back in good time to get changed too.

'We might as well go together,' he had said gruffly that morning.

Not perhaps the most romantic of invitations, but in spite of herself Martha's spirits were soaring. Once she would have turned up her nose at the thought of a stuffy diplomatic reception, but it had been so long since she had been anywhere or had a chance to dress up that she felt ridiculously excited at the thought of going out.

She had brought her favourite dress from her days at *Glitz*. Whenever they did a feature on 'My best buy ever' or 'The one piece of my wardrobe I would grab if there was a fire', Martha's dress would make an appearance. It had cost her a ridiculous amount of money, even with the generous discount the designer had given her because she had featured his clothes in *Glitz*, and on the hanger it looked no different from any chainstore dress.

The moment she slipped it on, though…ah, that was a very different matter! The whisper-soft material draped beautifully and never creased, and Martha felt fabulous whenever she wore it. Fashion editors famously wore black, but Martha's dress was a deep, dark gold that warmed her skin and flattered her figure. It was a deceptively simple sleeveless shift that you could wear to the most glamorous of A-list parties with heels and the perfect necklace, or with sandals to a casual bar by the beach.

This was the first time she had worn it since Noah was born, and it had lost none of its effect. Martha smoothed it down over her stomach and wriggled her feet into her kitten heels before twisting one way and another in front of the mirror. She had the strangest sensation that she had come face to face with her old self. With her make-up and her dress and her shoes to die for, she looked like a completely different person, the old Martha who had never cooed over prams or imagined that she would be happy to spend her days in a sarong and flip-flops.

She had been letting herself go, she told herself sternly. No wonder Candace thought she was mumsy.

Well, Candace would see a different Martha tonight! She would show her that she wasn't quite the downtrodden drudge that she imagined.

Lewis was talking to Eloise in the living room, but as Martha's door opened he broke off and turned. He was dressed in a white dinner jacket with a black bow tie, and he looked so austerely attractive that the breath snared in her throat. He seemed equally taken aback at the sight of her. The smile evaporated from his face and for a long moment he just stared in stunned disbelief.

Martha was conscious of a *frisson*, a tiny thrill at succeeding at last in shaking him out of that infuriating self-possession, but it vanished as she saw something oddly like disappointment flicker across his face before the slate eyes shuttered warily and his expression closed.

'You look…very…different,' he said in a voice empty of all expression.

Different? Was that all he could say? He might as well have come right out and said that he didn't like her like this. Obscurely hurt, Martha felt her confidence evaporate before a worse thought struck her.

What if he thought that she had gone to all this trouble for him? If it seemed as if she were angling for a repeat of that kiss? Remembering how horrified he had been when he realised that he was kissing her before, she thought with a sinking heart that it would certainly explain his wary look. He was probably terrified that she was planning to jump him again.

Mortified at the very thought, Martha felt a tide of colour wash up her neck, and the knowledge that she must look as humiliated as she felt only made her feel worse. She still had some pride, though, and gathered its meagre shreds together. Somehow she was just going to have to convince Lewis that kissing him again was the last thing she had in mind.

'Thank you,' she said with a brittle smile. 'I thought I should make an effort. You said all the Brits would be there tonight, so if there's even an outside chance that I might bump into Rory, then I want to make sure I'm looking my best.'

There was a tiny pause. 'Of course,' said Lewis roughly. 'I forgot that you were hoping to come across him.'

'Well, that's why I'm here, isn't it?' Martha managed another over-bright smile. If she said it often enough she might even remember it herself.

How could he have forgotten? How could he have been stupid enough to admit that he had? Lewis castigated himself savagely. It wasn't as if Martha had ever made a secret of why she was here or what she wanted.

He had just been shaken off balance by the way she looked when she came out of the bedroom, and it wasn't a feeling that he liked. He was used to her in a soft T-shirt that left her arms bare, or in her sarong, or in that man's shirt she wore at night, the one that was faded and slipped off her shoulder when she forgot about it. He didn't like her the way she looked now. She was too sophisticated like this, too glamorous, too eager to go out and party.

Lewis preferred her when she was in the kitchen, stirring pots, her face intent as she tasted a sauce, or sitting cross-legged on the floor, laughing as the babies tumbled against her. He liked her as a nanny, not a fashion editor.

But Martha didn't care what he liked, did she?

'We'd better go,' he said brusquely. 'We don't want to be late.'

The High Commission was an imposing colonial building set in immaculate grounds. Tonight was obviously one of the key social events of the year in Perpetua, and the gardens were crowded with people all dressed to the nines.

What if Rory was here after all? Martha viewed the throng with a sudden clutch of panic. What would she say to him? She had made such a fuss about him to Lewis that she couldn't simply ignore his presence. She would just have to hope that the idea of putting on a jacket would discourage Rory from attending the reception even if he had been invited. From what she remembered of him, that would be in character.

'Hello, there!' Candace had obviously been keeping an eye out for Lewis and intercepted him before he had a chance to disappear into the crowds. 'I was wondering when you'd get here.' She smiled at Lewis and laid a familiar hand on his arm. Martha wanted to smack it away.

'Hello,' she said clearly, and saw with satisfaction that Candace did a double take as she glanced at her.

'Martha!' The smug smile was wiped from her face as she took in the transformation, and she took her hand off Lewis, the icy blue eyes narrowing. 'I hardly recognised you.'

'I'm not in nanny mode tonight,' Martha agreed with an equally insincere smile. 'It's my night off.'

'Well…we must make sure you enjoy it, in that case.' Candace had made a quick recovery. 'Let me introduce you to a few people,' she offered in a blatant strategy to separate her from Lewis. Martha could practically see her thinking that while mumsy old Martha wasn't much of a rival, in that dress she might be more of a threat.

Martha could have told her she didn't have any reason to worry. Lewis had hardly said a word to her in the car. He either thought that she looked awful, or was so terrified that she was planning on jumping him again that he couldn't wait to fob her off on someone else. Either way, Martha had no intention of playing gooseberry to the two of them all evening. She put up her chin.

'That's sweet of you, but I've been to one or two parties before, and I think I can probably introduce myself.' She flashed Lewis a glittering smile. 'I'll no doubt see you later.'

Waggling her fingers at them both in her best *Glitz* style, she sashayed off, thanking God for her dress and her heels. She would never have been able to carry it off without them.

After so long as a virtual social recluse it was daunting at first to find herself isolated among complete strangers, but experience of all those parties she had been to in her twenties soon kicked in. Martha turned on the charm and before long was circulating as if she had been an integral part of Perpetua's social scene for years.

It would even have been fun if she hadn't been so aware of Lewis. She kept trying to move to a different part of the party, but wherever she was she seemed to be able to see him out of the corner of her eye, and no matter how hard she tried to ignore him it was as if her senses were fine-tuned to notice whenever he lifted a glass or turned his head.

It wasn't even as if he was making any effort, Martha noted crossly. Clearly not one of nature's party animals, he stood looking forbidding most of the time, and his smiles were perfunctory at best. Martha could almost have felt sorry for Candace, clinging so desperately to his arm. Surely even she could see that he wasn't enjoying himself?

Martha just wished that she wondered why Candace was bothering but, infuriatingly, she could see it all too easily. He made a formidable figure, she thought, watching him covertly as she pretended to listen to a long, involved story about a diving trip. It wasn't just those intimidating brows

or that austere look. It was something to do with the steely
self-containment, the air of cool competence that set him
apart from the crowd.

That and the fact that he was obviously hating this as a
waste of time. Why had he come at all? Martha wondered.
He could have stayed at home. He could be sitting on the
verandah right now, gazing out into the hot darkness and
listening to the ocean...

The longing to be there herself grabbed Martha out of
nowhere, like a hand gripping her heart, so hard and so
unexpected that she actually flinched—and, as if he had
heard her sharp, instinctive intake of breath, Lewis looked
across the garden and met her eyes.

For Martha, it was as if the ground between them had
suddenly opened up, leaving her teetering on the edge of
a yawning chasm. She didn't want to be here either, making polite chit-chat with strangers. She wanted to be on
the verandah too, and she wanted to be there with him.

'Are you OK?'

Belatedly, Martha realised that the man she was with
had broken off his story and was looking at her in some
concern. Wrenching her eyes away from Lewis's, she took
a gulp of her punch.

'Sorry...yes, I'm fine,' she said, but she didn't feel fine
at all. She felt sick and shaken with the enormity of what
she had just realised.

She wanted Lewis. There could be no future with him.
He wasn't the right father for Noah, and he wasn't the
right man for her, but she still wanted him in a way she
had never wanted anyone before. She wanted to go over
and push Candace away from him, to beg him to take her
out to the car and push her up against the door and kiss
her as he had kissed her that night. She wanted to drive
home through the tropical night, knowing that when they

got there she would be able to put her arms around him and burrow into his solid strength.

How much had Lewis seen as she stared at him? Martha felt giddy and disorientated, terrified that naked desire had been written all over her face, but when she risked another glance he was talking to the High Commissioner and looked perfectly normal. At least he didn't look as if his world had fallen apart the way hers had just done, and he wasn't backing out of the party, eyes rolling in search of escape, as he probably would have been doing if he had so much as an inkling of how she felt about him.

There was no use in fooling herself any longer. It was Lewis she wanted, Lewis she was in love with. It wasn't sensible, and it wasn't what she had wanted, but there wasn't anything she could do about it.

All she could do was try not to make a fool of herself and grope for her last shreds of pride. She had to keep remembering his expression when he had realised that he was kissing her, and the wariness that had crept into his eyes when he suspected that she had dressed up for him. The worst possible thing to do would be to tell him how she felt. He would just reject her out of hand, and then she and Noah would have to leave, and she would never see him or Viola again.

No, much better to keep her secret for now. There were months to go before her contract ran out, and a lot could happen in that time. Lewis might change his mind, might get used to having her around, might even think that he would miss her when she had gone.

For now, she just needed time alone to think about how she felt and what she was going to do. Her jaw was beginning to ache with the effort of smiling. She longed to go home but dreaded being alone with him before she had had time to get herself under control. As a result, when

Lewis came up to ask if she was ready to go home, Martha produced a brilliant smile.

'The party's hardly started,' she objected, as if she were having a wonderful time. As if her spine hadn't prickled with awareness of him walking up behind her. She hadn't been able to see him, but she had known that he was there.

'I don't want to leave Eloise too long,' said Lewis, who had evidently managed to shake off Candace at last. 'It's not fair on her.'

'I'm sure she wouldn't mind if we stayed a bit longer.'

He scowled. 'I'm not staying any longer. If you want a lift home, you'll have to come now.'

Martha wanted to put her arms around him and kiss the crossness away. How could she love him when he was so difficult? she asked herself in something close to despair, before pushing the feeling firmly away.

'I can always get a taxi,' she pointed out.

'I'll take you home if you like,' offered the man beside her. Martha had been too busy thinking about Lewis to notice him much, but she seemed to remember that he had been introduced as Peter.

His offer didn't go down well with Lewis, but Martha smiled at him. 'Would you really? That would be kind. Thank you *so* much.'

She turned back to Lewis, feeling better now that she didn't have to face the drive home in the dark with him. She wouldn't have to worry about keeping her hands under control, about the urge to touch him in the darkness, to break down and beg him to hold her.

'You go,' she said to Lewis. 'I'll be fine.'

'It's not you I'm worried about,' he said astringently. 'I was thinking more about Eloise. She might want to go home.'

'You're going to be there,' she pointed out, and his mouth tightened.

'It seems to have slipped your mind that I'm not the one employed as a nanny,' he snapped.

Martha hesitated. The only way she was going to get through this was to be as bolshie as possible, and with any luck Lewis wouldn't guess the real reason for her reluctance to go home with him.

'Excuse me,' she said to Peter with a martyred sigh. 'I've just been reminded who pays my wages. It looks as if I'm going to have to go.'

'Spare me the martyr act!' said Lewis, visibly irritated. 'If you're so determined to stay, you'd better stay. Don't mind me.'

'Fine, I won't,' said Martha childishly. It was bizarre how he could make her so cross and make her want to throw herself into his arms and beg him to take her with him at one and the same time.

She should have felt relieved to see Lewis stomp off, but she had to stop herself running after him. Now she just had to face hours of purgatory, pretending to have a great time with Peter. She hadn't registered just how pleased he was at the prospect, or envisaged that he would insist on taking her to Perpetua's only nightclub. Once Martha would have been the last person off the dance floor, but now she just wanted to go home, and she couldn't ask after making such a fuss with Lewis.

It was nearly two before Peter drove her back to the house. She was rather dreading it, in case he was expecting to round off the evening with some physical demonstration of her gratitude for possibly the worst four hours of her life, but there was no chance of that when Lewis loomed up on the verandah as the car came to a halt and stood glowering down at them.

'I think I'd better go,' Martha said to Peter, reaching for the door handle with barely concealed relief. 'Thanks for a lovely evening.'

'Where have you been?' Lewis demanded as she climbed the verandah steps wearily and a disconsolate Peter drove off.

'I've been checking out Perpetua's night life.'

'Until two in the morning?'

'That's the thing about night life—it usually happens at night,' Martha confided sarcastically. 'I realise that for you a night out is over at ten o'clock, but for the rest of us things don't get going until after midnight.'

'You could have rung and let me know that you weren't coming back after the reception,' Lewis growled.

'I could have done, but I didn't,' she said, walking past him into the living room. 'A—I thought you'd be in bed, and B—I don't have to account to you for what I do in my free time!'

'I could hardly go to bed until you got home,' he countered furiously. 'I didn't know where you were, or who you were with, or what you were doing. What if I'd needed to get in touch with you?'

Martha perched on an arm of the sofa and eased off her shoes. 'Why would you need to do that?'

'There might have been a problem with Viola or Noah,' said Lewis after a moment.

'Was there?'

'No,' he admitted grudgingly.

'I tell you what,' said Martha, wincing as she rubbed her sore feet. Fab as her shoes were, they weren't made for standing up in for long periods, and certainly not for dancing. 'Next time I go out, I'll check in with you on the hour, every hour. How about that?'

Lewis scowled at her facetiousness. 'What do you mean, *next time*?' he demanded. 'Are you seeing that Peter again?'

Martha flirted with the idea of pretending to have a passionate attraction for the poor, unsuspecting Peter, but decided that she wouldn't be able to carry it off.

'We haven't arranged anything, but I might do,' she said as airily as she could. 'He seemed very nice,' she added provocatively.

Lewis's brows were drawn into one fearsome bridge across his nose. 'I thought you were supposed to be looking for Noah's father?'

'I am, but I didn't meet anybody who knew him tonight.'

'And in the meantime you're keeping an eye out for substitutes, I suppose!' Hunching his shoulders, he prowled restlessly around the room as Martha stared at him furiously.

'What do you mean by that?'

'I saw the way you were chatting up all the men at that reception tonight,' he accused her. 'It looked as if you were working on a fall-back plan in case Rory doesn't appear to sign up for the father thing!'

Martha's eyes flashed dangerously. 'My son deserves better than a fall-back plan! He deserves the best father there is. It might not turn out to be his biological father, but I'm certainly not reduced to trawling round receptions in case I might find someone suitable for the *father thing* as you call it!'

'So what was the point of all that flirting?'

'I wasn't flirting. You and Candace made it very obvious that I was cramping your style, so I left you to your own devices. As far as I was concerned, I was just being pleasant.'

'Pleasant?' Still pacing, Lewis flung the word back at her over his shoulder. 'What does that mean, exactly?'

'Well, I haven't looked it up in a dictionary for a while,' said Martha, holding on to her own temper with difficulty, 'but I think it means smiling and being polite and showing an interest in other people, which was exactly what I was doing. And, frankly, I don't see what it has to do with you in any case!'

There was a pause. Lewis stopped to look at her, and then away. 'I didn't like it,' he said as if the words had been forced out of him. 'I didn't like the idea of you being interested in those other men, and I didn't like them being interested in you. I was jealous,' he added simply. 'I wanted you to be pleasant to *me*.'

It was so unexpected that Martha could only stare at him for a moment, not sure that she had heard him properly. 'Why?' she asked foolishly.

'Why? Look at you!' Lewis turned almost angrily. 'What man wouldn't want you? You look stunning.'

She opened her mouth, then closed it again. 'I didn't think you liked this dress,' was all she could say at last.

'It's not the dress.' He shrugged his shoulders in an odd gesture of defeat. 'The truth is that I didn't like the fact that you wanted to go out. It was childish of me, I know,' he added heavily. 'I wanted you to stay here with me.'

Martha shook her head in incomprehension. 'Why?' she said again, wishing she could think of something perceptive or witty to say instead.

He came over then and took the shoes from her hand, letting them drop on to the wooden floor. 'Why do you think?' he asked, and the look in his eyes set Martha's heart slamming painfully against her ribs.

Her throat was too dry for her to speak. She could only look helplessly up at him, pinioned by the warmth of his gaze, paralysed by the fear that if she moved she would break the moment and that time would rewind, leaving Lewis on the other side of the room, not standing right next to her, watching her with that expression that dissolved her bones and flooded her with warmth.

'I think you know why,' he said softly when she didn't

answer. 'I think you know that I haven't been able to stop thinking about how it felt to kiss you, about what it would be like to kiss you again. Every time I see you in that shirt you wear at night I want to take it off you. I want to undo the buttons very slowly and pull it from your shoulders. I want to touch you the way I touched you that night, the way I would have gone on touching you if Viola hadn't cried.'

Martha moistened her lips and found her voice at last. 'But you seemed so horrified, as if you didn't even realise it was me you were kissing.'

'I knew it was you all right,' he said with a twisted smile. 'It wasn't the first time I'd thought about kissing you, but I knew that I shouldn't. You weren't in any position to resist, and I was ashamed of myself for taking advantage of you. I shouldn't have done it.'

'What if I liked being taken advantage of?' said Martha a little shakily. She looked up at him with dark, direct eyes. 'What if I wanted you to take advantage of me?'

'Did you?' Lewis's voice wasn't that steady either. He swallowed. 'Do you?'

She let out a breath, suddenly certain. This wasn't about the future. It was about what she wanted now. She wanted to forget about the future, not for ever, but for now. She didn't want to think about anything but Lewis and the promise in his eyes and how his hands and his mouth and his body would feel against hers.

'Yes,' she said. 'Yes, to both.' And the blaze of expression in his face sent a thrill through her.

He took her hands in his and drew her to her feet. 'Are you sure, Martha?'

Martha's fingers tightened around his and she smiled. 'I'm sure. Are you?'

'Am I sure?' Lewis was shaken by a silent laugh. 'When I've been thinking about this for so long? Yes, I'm sure.'

And then their smiles faded as he bent his head and their lips met at last in a soft kiss that caught and clung and went on and on until they broke apart at last for breath. Lewis's hands slid up to tangle in her silky hair. 'God, yes, I'm sure,' he said raggedly, and then there was no more talking for a very, very long time.

When Martha woke the next morning she was pressed against Lewis's warm, solid back. He was lying with his face buried in the pillow, apparently still asleep, and she kissed the back of his neck where it was irresistibly close to her mouth.

He stirred slightly but didn't move, so she kissed him again, letting her lips drift along his bare shoulder.

Still no response. Piqued, Martha lifted herself up and applied herself to the task more seriously. Starting at the base of his neck, she pressed seductively soft kisses around and up to the lobe of his ear, over the rough prickle of his jaw, and on to linger at the corner of his mouth.

'Are you awake?' she whispered, encouraged by an infinitesimal twitch of his lips.

'No,' said Lewis, barely moving his lips.

'Not even a little bit?'

The dent at the corner of his mouth deepened. 'No,' he said again, and then took her by surprise, rolling over suddenly to pin her beneath him and kiss her. 'But I get the feeling I'm going to be waking up any minute now!'

Martha smiled with satisfaction and stretched beneath his hands. 'What time is it?' she asked lazily.

Lewis raised himself slightly to squint at the clock on the bedside table. 'Too early to get up,' he said, and settled comfortably back on top of her, his face resting in the curve of her throat. 'The babies will still be sound asleep.'

'I'm sorry I woke you in that case,' she said, winding

her arms around his back. 'Do you want to go back to sleep?'

There was a pause, just long enough for her to wonder if he had done just that, and then she felt him smile against her skin. 'I don't think I can now,' he said, as his lips drifted downwards. 'How about you? Are you sleepy?'

'No.' Martha caught her breath as his hands traced possessive patterns over her. 'No, not at all.'

CHAPTER NINE

IT WAS the beginning of a golden time for Martha. In some ways nothing had changed. Lewis still went to work every day, she still did the cooking, the babies still needed their nappies changed and their noses wiped and the Indian Ocean still surged against the reef beyond the lagoon.

But in other ways, everything was different. Martha had never felt so fulfilled, so complete, so *alive*. She hadn't known happiness as such a physical sensation before. It tingled at the ends of her fingers and quivered deep inside her, whenever she looked at the two babies, growing browner and bonnier by the day, when she stood on the verandah and caught a glimpse of the sea glittering through the palms, when she woke up every morning next to Lewis and could run her hand luxuriously over his flat stomach and his broad chest, could press her lips against him and smell the scent of his skin and taste his mouth.

He had relaxed in a way she wouldn't have been able to imagine when they first arrived in St Bonaventure. Sometimes Martha would watch him smiling at the babies, and her heart seemed to turn inside out. When he came home he would kiss her unselfconsciously, and scoop up Noah or Viola and toss them in the air until they squealed with delight, and she would feel dizzy with love for him.

Later, when the babies were asleep, they would sit on the verandah and talk, but too often Martha would lose track of the conversation as she thought about the night to come and shivered with delight, knowing that all it would take would be for her to turn her head and smile and Lewis would pull her on to his lap, that she could reach out when-

149

ever she wanted and touch him, that when they couldn't wait any longer he would take her to bed and make love to her.

They never talked about the future. If she found herself wondering what would happen at the end of the six months, Martha would push the thought away. She didn't want to think about it. She only wanted to think about now. Lewis seemed so happy too that she let herself hope that he might be coming round to the idea of family life—the *father thing*, as he had called it—after all, but she was afraid to ask when he didn't mention it. At the back of her mind she knew that she still needed to find Rory, that he deserved to know that he had a son, and that Noah would need to know his father, but there was no hurry, was there? All that mattered was now.

So Martha closed her mind to everything but the present. She was happy, Noah was happy. She couldn't ask for more than that.

'How would you feel about having another dinner party?' Lewis asked her one day, kissing the side of her neck as she stirred a pot on the stove and sending a shiver of sheer pleasure down her spine.

Martha smiled at the sensation. 'Who did you want to invite?' she asked, not without some difficulty as his arms were around her waist and his lips were distracting her.

'The resident engineer and his wife, the office manager and a couple of the local contractors. I thought we could ask Candace as well,' he added casually.

'Candace?' Martha bristled in spite of herself. 'Why her?'

'She's got some useful contacts,' he told her. 'She's been very helpful in one way and another.'

Martha had no problem imagining that! Pressing her lips together, she moved out of the circle of Lewis's arms and pretended to be consulting her recipe.

'Martha, you're not jealous of Candace by any chance, are you?' There was an undercurrent of laughter in his voice that sent warmth seeping along her bones.

'No,' she lied, steeling herself against it, but then she met his eyes and relented. 'Well, maybe a bit,' she conceded. 'She's just so perfect.'

Lewis turned her back to face him and held her firmly by the waist. 'She's not perfect for me,' he said. 'You know there's no need for you to be jealous of Candace, really, don't you?'

Martha looked into his face, and what she read there made her heart contract. No man could look at her like that if he had any interest at all in another woman, least of all a man like Lewis. She was being silly.

'Yes,' she said, 'I know.'

It didn't mean that she was looking forward to meeting Candace again, though. At least dinner wasn't the disaster it had been the last time, and she had things much more under control. There was even time to change before the guests arrived, but Martha was chagrined to find that she was still intimidated by Candace's icy perfection. She could forget about her fashion editor past. Whatever she wore now, and whatever she did, she was tarred with the slightly scruffy, chaotic brush of motherhood and it was impossible to remove.

Oh, well, thought Martha. If she had to choose between being perfect and being a mother, she knew which one she would choose every time. It would just be nice if she could be both occasionally.

Without discussing it, she and Lewis made an effort to behave as if nothing had changed between them. There were certainly no 'darlings' or kisses blown across the table—neither of which would have been Lewis's style, or hers, come to that—but Candace still picked up on the current of awareness between them immediately. Martha saw the glacial blue eyes narrow as she looked from one to the other.

Candace didn't say anything, but the first lull in the conversation gave her the opportunity she had been waiting for, and she leant across her neighbour and asked Martha very clearly whether she had managed to track down Rory yet.

Martha glanced at Lewis, and saw with a sinking heart that the old guarded look had clanged back into place at the mention of Rory. If Candace's object had been to remind him of Martha's original intentions, she had obviously succeeded.

'No, not yet,' she said after a moment.

'It's a very romantic story,' Candace told the other guests. 'Martha lost touch with her baby's father, but she's come out here specifically to find him, so you must all let her know if you come across any marine biologists.'

Which, as a way of suggesting that Martha slept around casually, carelessly got herself pregnant and then pursued Rory across continents, having not bothered to keep in touch with him before, wasn't bad, Martha told herself wryly. Candace was quite an expert. If nothing else, she was obviously determined to get Martha out of Lewis's life as soon and as permanently as possible. If Martha had felt more sure of Lewis it would have been funny. As it was, she had a nasty feeling that some of Candace's needling remarks might be hitting home.

Not receiving any encouragement to pursue the theme of Martha as a feckless mother, Candace sought around for another subject that might discomfit her, settling at last on that old favourite—children. She did it very cleverly too, pretending to admire Martha for her patience while subtly reminding her audience—Lewis—of how messy and demanding babies were, before moving on to ask him delicately if he was expecting to hear from his sister soon.

'I'm sure Savannah must be eager to have her baby back as soon as possible,' she said. 'I must say I think you've been marvellous, Lewis, coping with all that extra responsibility when you've got this big project on.'

'It's Martha who's been coping with Viola,' he said, but Candace seemed oddly oblivious to the curtness in his voice.

'Oh, I know she's a wonderful nanny,' she agreed, putting Martha firmly in her place, 'but it's still been a bit of an imposition, hasn't it? I remember how much I sympathised when you told me how important it was for you to feel that your home was quiet and ordered, and you never get that with a baby around, do you?'

She didn't quite come out and remind him that he would have his perfect life back the moment he got rid of Viola, and therefore any need for Martha and Noah to hang around, but she might as well have done, thought Martha. Lewis was looking withdrawn, and she was afraid that Candace had had exactly the effect she wanted.

A little chill crept into Martha's heart. They had been so happy. Surely Candace couldn't spoil everything that easily?

She dreaded the moment when all the guests would leave, imagining how Lewis would be remembering how his life used to be, but when he had closed the door after the last of them had gone he only sighed with relief.

Martha was gathering up coffee cups and bracing herself for him to tell her that he didn't want to get any more involved, so convinced of what his reaction would be that when he came over to take her hands she was quite unprepared for what he actually said.

'Leave them,' said Lewis. 'We can do that in the morning. Let's go to bed.'

He didn't say anything else, but he made love to her

with an urgency that left Martha shaken with a mixture of
fulfilment and concern.

'What is it?' she asked softly as they lay together afterwards.

'Nothing,' he said.

He couldn't explain to her how he had felt as Candace's
voice went on and on, how much he had wished that she
would just shut up. He hadn't wanted to be reminded about
Rory, and he certainly hadn't wanted to think about the
future, but Candace had forced him to face the prospect of
life without Martha and the babies.

For the first time Lewis had questioned what he really
wanted. It wasn't that he was in love with Martha—he was
too old for all that stuff—but he liked her and he desired
her and he felt comfortable with her. That wasn't the same
as being ready to settle down, take on responsibility for
Noah and spend the rest of his life with her, was it?

No, it wasn't love. It was just that he couldn't imagine
how it would be without them. What it would be like to
come home at the end of the day to an empty house.

That was how it would be if Savannah did turn up to
claim Viola, and he wouldn't put it past her to do just that.
Jumping on a plane and demanding her baby back was
exactly the kind of thing his sister did on a whim. It wasn't
so long ago that Lewis would have welcomed her, but he
had a nasty feeling that if she rang him now to say that
she was on her way the bottom would fall out of his world.

Of course, that didn't mean that he wanted to look after
Viola for ever. It didn't mean that he wanted Martha to
stay for ever. It meant that he wanted... The fact was,
Lewis didn't *know* what he wanted any more. He just knew
that he felt restless and unsettled, and he didn't like it.

Nothing had changed, he tried to reassure himself.
Martha would be as reluctant to get too involved as he
was. As Candace had reminded him, she had made it very

clear that she was in search of a father for Noah, and he wasn't prepared to fulfil that role, so if their six months were up with no sign of Rory, she would say goodbye.

And that would be that.

Without meaning to, his arms tightened around Martha. 'Are you happy?' he asked her almost fiercely.

She eased herself above him so that she could look down into his face, studying him with her dark eyes, her silky hair swinging softly against his cheek. 'Right now?' she said, and bent down to kiss him. 'Yes,' she murmured against his mouth, 'I am.'

And she *was*, Martha told herself later, suppressing the tiny niggle of doubt about the future. Lewis evidently didn't want to think about what would happen then, and neither did she.

So they both carried on not thinking about it, and as the days passed, and then the weeks, it became more and more difficult to broach the subject. It was easier to push the thought aside, to decide that they would deal with the future when it came and not before.

Until the afternoon Candace turned up on the front verandah.

'I was just passing,' she said. 'I thought I'd drop in and say hello.'

Martha couldn't hide her surprise. 'Lewis is still at work,' she said, hoping she was more successful at masking her dislike. 'He won't be back until a bit later.'

Candace waved an airy hand. 'It's you I came to see,' she said.

After that, Martha didn't have much choice but to ask her in for a drink. They made stilted conversation as she made some tea and took it out on to the verandah, where she installed Viola and Noah in their high chairs and gave them a rusk each to keep them quiet.

'I felt I had to come out and congratulate you,' said

Candace, averting her eyes from the way Viola was smearing her soggy biscuit over the tray.

Martha was busy rescuing Noah's as it threatened to fall on to the floor, so she thought she must have misheard.

'Sorry, congratulate who?' she asked when Noah was happily sucking his biscuit once more.

'You.' Candace beamed at her in a way that Martha found oddly chilling. 'You must be thrilled!'

A nasty feeling was beginning to uncurl inside Martha. She didn't know what was coming, but she knew she wasn't going to like it.

'I'm sure I would be if I knew what you were talking about,' she said.

'Why, finding Noah's father, of course!'

There was a frozen pause. 'Rory?' said Martha carefully.

'Yes, Rory McMillan. It is him, isn't it?' Candace settled back in her chair, enjoying the effect her words were having. 'What a coincidence, him turning out to be part of the team that Lewis is using for the environmental study for the port!'

Yes, what a coincidence, thought Martha grimly. 'Where did you meet him?'

'Oh, I haven't actually met him myself,' said Candace with obvious regret. 'I gather there are a group of them over here, and they all came into the bar at the hotel the other day. By the time I'd realised that they were working on a marine project, Rory had left, apparently, but I asked if they knew of him, of course, and that's when they told me he was working for Lewis.'

She glanced slyly at Martha, who was doing her damnedest not to give her the satisfaction of reacting the way she really wanted to react. Beginning with killing Lewis. Or possibly Candace, and then Lewis. The possibilities were endless, when you came to think of it.

'I would have asked them to pass a message on to Rory, asking him to get in touch with you, but I knew that if he was working for Lewis then of course Lewis would know all about him anyway, and tell you.'

'Of course,' said Martha through her teeth.

Except that he hadn't told her, had he?

When Lewis came back that night he could see at once that something was wrong. Martha was holding herself rigidly, and she was as taut as a suspension cable on one of his bridges, but she refused to talk until the babies were safely in bed.

'So, are you going to tell me what's wrong now?' he asked as she shut the bedroom door gently behind her.

'I am indeed,' said Martha, walking into the living room and folding her arms in an effort to keep herself under control. She was so angry that she was afraid she would cry. That or throw something.

She turned to face Lewis from a safe distance. 'I understand that you've taken on some marine biologists to do a study of the environmental effects of building the port?'

Lewis's expression froze. This was the moment that he had been dreading. 'Yes,' he said, still hoping against hope that she didn't know the whole truth.

'And one of them is called Rory McMillan?'

Well, he had known that it was a pretty futile hope. Deep down, he had known from the moment he walked in this evening. 'Yes,' he said.

'The very same Rory McMillan I've been trying to contact ever since I came here?'

She hadn't been trying that hard, Lewis thought with a flare of resentment, but decided that it would be wiser not to say it at this stage. 'Who told you?' he asked instead, which turned out to be just as bad.

Martha's eyes were bright with temper. 'Not the person

who should have done, obviously! As it was, I had to hear the good news from your friend Candace. She couldn't wait to get over here and congratulate me on my good fortune.'

'Candace?' Lewis frowned. 'How did she know?'

'I don't think that's the point, is it, Lewis? The real point is that you knew and you didn't tell me.'

Couldn't he *see* that? Couldn't he tell how much that hurt? Martha hugged her arms together and forced back the tears, swallowing the hard, angry lump in her throat. 'How long have you known Rory?'

'I don't really know him,' said Lewis defensively. 'I just talked to the project leader, some guy called Steve. Surveys like the one we need for the port give their projects extra income to fund research, so he was willing to send a couple of his marine biologists along. They just introduced themselves as John and Rory. I didn't know it was him for sure.'

'But you had a good idea?'

'Yes,' he admitted, remembering the sick feeling of recognition as Rory had strolled into the office. *Gorgeous*, Martha had called him. *Tall, tanned, blond, dancing blue eyes*. Lewis didn't know about gorgeous, but the rest of her description had fitted pretty well. Personally, he had disliked Rory on sight. He was too cocky by half.

'How long ago was this?' Martha asked, with the same stony expression.

Lewis sighed. 'About ten days.'

'Ten days?' Unable to stand still, Martha took a turn around the room while she struggled with the urge to have the kind of tantrum Viola indulged in with such effect. 'Why didn't you *tell* me?'

Why *hadn't* he told her? Lewis asked himself. It was hard to explain now his sick, shameful feeling that had been perilously close to panic. The realisation that those weeks with Martha would end after all. The fear that she would take one look at Rory and fall for him all over again.

Lewis was under no illusions about how he would compare to Rory. The other man was young and good-looking, and had the sort of breezy, careless charm that he had never been able to master. On top of which, Rory was Noah's father. What did *he* have to offer compared to that?

Unable to admit just how afraid he was that Martha would simply take Noah and leave him for Rory, Lewis had let himself believe that there was no need for her to know yet. He had planned to tell her when Rory was safely back on his atoll, so that she could contact him when the six months was up.

'I was going to tell you,' he said to Martha, although it was hard to talk to her when she was stalking around like that. 'The time just never seemed right.' That sounded lame, even to his own ears. 'I wanted Rory to concentrate on the study. There's a deadline for that, and it's not as if you needed to contact him urgently.'

'Oh, yes, we mustn't forget the *study*, must we?' She rounded on him. 'I'm *so* glad you thought of that! Forget the fact that you knew Rory was the reason I came here in the first place!'

Lewis could feel himself being driven into a corner. Everything he said just seemed to make things worse. What was it about Martha that made him lose his cool? He was famous for his ability to sort out crises on site, for his relentless control in the most fraught of negotiations. Now look at him, stumbling over explanations like a fool!

'Viola wasn't well,' he tried, 'and you had a lot of things on your mind.'

'Yes, and one of them was finding Noah's father! I think I could have coped with a bit of good news!'

'I didn't know if it *would* be good news,' Lewis was provoked into saying.

At least that got her to stop pacing. She stared at him furiously. 'What do you mean by that?'

'You said you were happy,' he reminded her deliberately, and she turned her face away.

'That was before I knew you were capable of keeping something this important from me.'

Lewis set his jaw. He had made such a mess of it he might as well go on. 'And I'm not sure Rory would be a good father for Noah,' he told her. 'He seems very young to me, and very casual about everything. I couldn't see him changing nappies. From what I can gather, he keeps the bars going when he's here, and spends the rest of his time on the project which is based on a tiny uninhabited island. An atoll isn't a suitable place to bring up a baby.'

'It's not for you to decide who would or wouldn't be a good father for Noah!' Martha eyed him with freezing scorn. 'The fact is that Rory *is* his father, and there's nothing you or I or anyone else can do about it. And frankly,' she swept on, 'you're not exactly in a strong position to criticise when it comes to fatherhood either, are you? The chances are that Rory would make a better father than you. At least he doesn't lie!'

There was a white shade around Lewis's mouth. 'I haven't lied.'

'Oh, so when I asked you if anything interesting had happened during your day, the way I always do when you get home, and you didn't tell me that you had bumped into the father of my baby, the very man I've spent months trying to track down, you didn't think that it was a lie when you said "no"?'

Lewis dropped on to one of the chairs and rested his elbows on his knees, raking his fingers through his hair with a sigh. 'Look, I'm sorry,' he said after a fraught silence, 'but it's not the end of the world, is it? Rory's not going anywhere. You wanted to know how to contact him, and now you do. I don't understand what the problem is.'

He didn't understand? Martha stared at him in disbelief. That made them equal then. It was like trying to talk to someone from a different planet. Maybe there was something in this Venus and Mars stuff after all.

'You make it sound as if I'm making a big fuss about nothing,' she said tightly. 'Can't you imagine what it was like for me to hear about Rory from Candace? She just sat there, *gloating*! She knew you hadn't told me anything. Have you any idea how humiliating that felt?'

In spite of herself, her voice wobbled, and she drew a steadying breath. 'Have you got any idea what it feels like to discover that the man you—' she nearly said 'love' but checked herself just in time '—the man you've been sleeping with, the man you've *trusted*, turns out to be arrogant and deceitful and selfish enough to keep something so important from you, and then *stupid* enough not to understand why you're angry?'

Even in the white-hot flame of her fury Martha held on to the thought that if he would just say that he hadn't told her because he was afraid of losing her it might be all right.

But Lewis didn't say that.

'I didn't want you to forget that you're here on a contract,' he said instead. 'How would I cope with Viola if you were chasing around after Rory McMillan?'

The contract? Was that all he cared about? Hurt tore across Martha's heart and stung her eyes. He had never mentioned love, it was true, but she had thought that she meant more to him than that.

'Don't worry, I'm in no danger of forgetting my contract,' she said tightly. 'But there's nothing in it to say that I can't make contact with Rory before the six months is up.' She stopped as a horn sounded aside. 'Talking of which, that'll be my taxi.'

Taxi? What taxi? Lewis watched Martha cross the room to pick up her bag with a mixture of fear and frustration. 'Where are you going?'

'I'm going to find Rory and talk to him.'

'Now?' he demanded, getting to his feet.

'Yes, now. I wouldn't dream of interrupting while he's working on your precious survey, so the evening is the best time to find him. You said that he spends his spare time in bars, so it shouldn't be too hard to track him down. The town's not that big.'

Lewis could feel himself flailing. 'What about the babies?'

'You can babysit,' she told him. 'I would have thought it's the least you can do, in the circumstances!'

She was walking away; her hand was on the door. Lewis looked at her with a kind of desperation. He wanted to go after her, to push the door back into place, to beg her to stay, but she was too angry. She wouldn't believe anything he said now.

He swallowed. 'When will you be back?' he heard himself ask, as if from a great distance.

'When I've talked to Rory.' Martha turned at the door, and her expression was colder than he had ever seen it. 'Don't wait up.' Then the door had closed behind her, and she was gone.

Rory was in the third bar she tried. He was sitting at a table with several others, all dressed in shorts and casual tops. They were all young, all tanned, all glowing with health and vitality. They looked as if they were waiting to audition for *Baywatch*.

Martha hesitated, watching Rory across the room. It was hard to imagine anyone more different from Lewis. He looked younger even than she had remembered, but the blue-eyed charm was still plainly in evidence as he flirted with a very pretty girl, as blonde as he was, who kept tossing her hair back and laughing just a little too loudly.

Maybe this wasn't a good time? Rory was obviously otherwise occupied and, judging by her body language, the girl wouldn't welcome an interruption either.

But, then, there was never going to be a good time, was there? And her alternative was to go home to Lewis. Deep down, the thought of doing just that was so appealing that Martha wavered, before she stiffened her spine with the memory of the reasons he had given for keeping her in the dark. The environmental study. That contract. How could she go back to him now and admit that she hadn't even talked to Rory?

So Martha took a deep breath, squared her shoulders and walked across the bar to Rory's table. 'Hello, Rory,' she said.

Rory looked up, his blank expression replaced after a couple of seconds by one of ludicrous amazement. *'Martha?'*

'Well, that's good,' said Martha, forcing a smile. 'I wasn't sure if you'd remember me at all.'

'Of course I do!' Rory leapt to his feet, beaming. 'Hey, it's great to see you!' He gave her a big, unselfconscious hug, and then held her away from him, still shaking his head in surprise. 'You're the last person I expected to see here! I just didn't recognise you at first. You look so different!'

'Do I?' said Martha, a little taken aback. 'How?'

But Rory was already reaching for a chair and urging her to sit down, waving at the waitress to bring another beer. 'Move up, everyone,' he said, making room for her beside him, and although the blonde girl masked her disappointment quickly Martha caught a flash of resentment and felt uncomfortable. She hadn't thought about what impact her news would have on anyone else, she realised guiltily.

'Meet Martha, everybody.' Rory ran through the names of the others round the table, although the only one that registered with Martha was the girl, who was called Amy. 'I met Martha when I was in London last year,' he continued proudly. 'She's a fashion editor and has an incredibly glamorous lifestyle.'

Nobody said anything, but the looks of polite disbelief around the table told Martha just how much she had changed since coming to St Bonaventure. She had been so angry that she hadn't stopped to change or put on any make-up, and now she felt horribly conscious of the crow's-feet around her eyes and strands of grey in her dark hair. She always pulled them out when she saw them, but today had been the kind of day that put them all back.

'So, what are you doing here, Martha?' Rory asked, turning to her, his handsome face lit up with a kind of puppyish enthusiasm.

'I'm…working,' she said carefully.

'Bikinis on the beach, all that kind of thing? Cool.'

'Not exactly,' said Martha, as her beer arrived. She didn't want one, but she took a sip anyway. 'Actually, I'm here as a nanny.'

There was a pause, and then Rory burst out laughing. 'You're kidding, right? I can't imagine you with kids!'

Martha kept the smile on her face with difficulty. 'It's true.'

He stared at her. 'I always thought you were so cool,' he said, baffled. 'Why would you give up a great career like that to be a *nanny*?'

Her hands tightened in her lap and she forced herself to relax them. Be fair, she told herself. You used to think that looking after children would be the pits, too.

'Perhaps I fancied a career change,' she said.

Rory shook his head, still struggling with the idea of her change of image. He obviously hadn't entirely given up on the idea that she might be pulling his leg. 'Are you really a nanny?'

'Yes.' Martha took a breath. 'In fact, I think you know who I'm working for—Lewis Mansfield?' It hurt just to say his name.

'Lewis? Yeah, I know him all right.' Rory grinned and rolled his eyes. 'That's one scary guy! Does he ever smile?'

Martha thought about the way he smiled as he pulled her on to his lap. The way he smiled as he carried Noah into the sea, the sunlight reflected from the water rocking over their skins. The way he smiled against her skin.

She swallowed. Crying now would *not* be a good idea. 'Sometimes,' she said.

'He certainly doesn't smile at me,' said Rory, picking up his beer. 'I don't think he likes me.'

'Oh, come on,' said Amy, bang on cue. 'Why on earth wouldn't he like you?'

'Jealous of my legendary charm, perhaps?' Rory joked. 'What do you think, Martha? You must know him quite well.'

'Quite well, yes,' said Martha with a tight feeling in her chest.

'He's not the matiest of blokes, is he? He reminds me of my old maths teacher. Talk about grim!'

'Yeah,' agreed someone else. 'Only in my case it was geography. When he fixes you with that look you feel like you're twelve and he's about to give you a detention for talking at the back of the class!'

They all laughed, and Martha bit her lip.

'It just takes a little while to get to know him, that's all,' she said.

She couldn't bear it. She didn't want to be here in this loud bar, with these young, trendy people, listening to them mock Lewis. They didn't know him. They had no idea what he was like.

She wasn't going to be able to talk to Rory here, anyway. She could hardly announce his fatherhood in front of this audience. Quite apart from anything else, she would have to shout to make herself heard over the music. That wasn't the way she wanted to introduce the idea of Noah to his father.

So she carried on smiling, finished her beer, then said that she had to go. 'But it would be great to catch up with you properly,' she said to Rory as he got to his feet to say goodbye. 'What about lunch tomorrow?'

'Sure,' he said, surprised but pleased. He put his arm round her and gave her a hug. 'You know, it's really good to see you again, Martha. I often think about that time in London. We had a good time, didn't we?'

'Yes.' Martha disengaged herself as unobtrusively as she could. She knew that she ought to be delighted that he seemed so pleased to see her, but right now the thought of him wanting to pick up their previous relationship was downright unnerving. It wasn't that he wasn't attractive. He was.

He just wasn't Lewis.

CHAPTER TEN

MARTHA took Noah with her to lunch the next day, and made sure that they were there early so that they had a quiet table. Rory wasn't unduly surprised to see her with a baby, and gave Noah a careless pat as he sat down.

'So you really are a nanny! Is this your charge?'

'You could say that,' said Martha. 'This is Noah. He's my son.'

'Your *son*?'

She could see him assessing Noah's age and doing some rapid calculations. He was a biologist, after all, and he wasn't stupid. His face changed.

'Yes,' she told him gently, knowing that he had already worked it all out. 'Noah's your son, too.'

At first Rory was too shell-shocked to take much in. He kept staring at Noah as if he couldn't quite believe that he was a real baby, and it took some time for Martha to convince him that she wasn't interested in financial support. 'It's not about money,' she insisted. 'I just want Noah to know who his father is.'

Rory relaxed once the prospect of handing over a share of his grant had been removed, and as he got used to the idea of being a father he became positively enthusiastic.

Once, Martha had found that puppyish enthusiasm endearing, but now it seemed naïve. Unlike Lewis, Rory obviously had no idea what was involved in looking after a baby, but she couldn't discourage him, not after coming this far, and when Rory suggested that she and Noah move in with him for a while she felt trapped.

'The others are going back to the project site tomorrow,

but I'm staying on to finish the survey on the port,' he was explaining. 'I'll be here for another month or so, and I'll have the project house to myself. You and Noah could come and live with me and we could get to know each other properly.'

It should have been her dream scenario. Wasn't this exactly what she had wanted when she had first thought about coming out to St Bonaventure?

Martha told herself she ought to be thrilled that everything was working out so well. Rory had come round to the idea of fatherhood far more quickly than she had expected. He was saying all the right things, doing all the right things. He had Noah on his knee now and was making him chuckle. It was all perfect.

Only it didn't feel perfect. Martha didn't want to move in with him straight away. She didn't want to leave Viola. Or Lewis.

'That would be lovely, Rory,' she said dutifully, 'but we can't come straight away. I've got another baby to look after, and my contract lasts another couple of months.'

'I'll be back on the project then,' objected Rory. 'We just camp out there, so it would be hard with Noah. I'm sure we could work something out about the other baby. Why don't you ask Lewis, anyway?'

Noah's father, anxious to spend time with their son. How could she argue with that?

'All right,' said Martha. 'I'll ask him.'

'So, how was your lunch?' Lewis asked sardonically when he came home that night.

He had given himself a good talking to the night before and, having cursed himself for a fool at first, was now well on the way to persuading himself that this was all for the best. Things had been getting too cosy with Martha and the two babies. If they had gone on much longer he might easily have found himself sucked into the kind of commitment he had been so careful to avoid for so long.

Perhaps it was just as well that Rory had turned up when he did. Now all it needed was for Martha to have calmed down and they could end things in a civilised way.

Which was fine in theory, but less easy in practice, when he had spent the night before and all of that day torturing himself by thinking about Martha and Rory together.

'Lunch was fine,' said Martha. She had calmed down all right. Last night's fury had petered out and she was looking tired and strained. Lewis wanted to gather her into his arms and hold her until the tension drained out of her body.

Not that she would want to be comforted by someone arrogant, selfish and…what was it?…yes, deceitful. She might not be spitting sparks any more, but she wouldn't have forgotten.

Lewis looked away, steeling himself against the urge to go down on his knees and tell her that he was sorry, to beg her to forgive him and ask if they could go back to the way they were before. It was too late for that now.

'Did Rory acknowledge Noah as his son and heir?' he asked instead.

'Yes.' Martha drew a breath. 'He wanted us to spend the next couple of weeks with him, but I explained about Viola and the fact that I hadn't finished my contract yet.'

'Don't worry about it,' said Lewis, and only he knew what that careless shrug cost him. 'I guessed that's what you would want to do, so I've already spoken to Eloise, and she's agreed to look after Viola during the day.'

She swallowed. 'What about the evenings?'

'I'm sure I'll manage,' he said indifferently. 'I'm not completely useless, and it's not as if it's for much longer, anyway.'

'But…what about the contract?' said Martha, stricken.

He had gone on and on and *on* about that contract. How could he suddenly pretend that it didn't matter to him? She had been depending on him to insist that she and Noah stayed, and now it was as if he couldn't wait to get rid of her.

'Far be it from me to stand in the way of reuniting a happy family,' said Lewis, looking withdrawn. 'I'm not a monster. You've been very clear about what you wanted, and now that it looks as if things are working out for you I'd be unreasonable to insist on you fulfilling the terms of your contract.'

'Well…perhaps we could treat it as a few days off?' Martha was struggling not to sound desperate, but Lewis didn't seem to care one way or another.

'I'm sure you don't want to commit yourself to anything,' he said, his eyes shuttered. 'There's no telling what might happen. Rory might decide that he likes family life so much that he doesn't want to go back to the project. I'm going to try and contact Savannah tomorrow, too, and if she's ready to have Viola back I won't need you at all.'

That hurt more than anything. He wasn't even going to try and persuade her to stay, Martha realised bleakly.

It looked as if she didn't have much choice. She could hardly insist on remaining with Viola after everything that she had said last night, but saying goodbye to the baby was one of the hardest things she had ever done. She couldn't even explain why she was going. It made Martha realise just how much she had come to love Viola, and how much she was going to miss her.

And her stubborn, difficult uncle.

To the very last minute Martha let herself hope that Lewis would change his mind. Their last morning was bizarrely normal. Viola and Noah were up early, and she was in the kitchen giving them both breakfast as Lewis came in, hesitating only a second before he poured himself a cup of the coffee she had made the way she always did.

Martha closed her eyes and wished that she could re-wind time. That when she opened them again they would be back to where they had been before. Lewis would put down his cup and kiss her goodbye, and when he came home he would smile and toss the babies in the air, the way he always did.

But it wasn't going to happen that way. When he came home tonight she wouldn't be here. Martha felt sick at the thought.

No amount of wishing was going to change things now. Nothing could undo the fact that Lewis had lied to her, but if he would only ask her to stay she was sure that they could work something out.

Lewis gulped down his coffee and set down his cup. 'I have to go,' he said brusquely. His face was like a mask, but Martha saw his eyes rest on Noah and for a fleeting moment something flickered in his expression and was gone before he turned to her.

'Thanks for everything,' he said.

That was it? *Thanks for everything?* When Martha thought of the times they had shared, the sunlit mornings and the dark evenings on the verandah and the long, hot tropical nights, she wanted to throw something after him. The surge of anger was oddly comforting, though. It consumed her as she chucked her things into a case and dismantled Noah's cot, and stopped her from thinking about how much she was hurting.

She was furious with Lewis, but far more so with herself. Why had she let herself get so involved? She had known all along what he was like. She had known there would be no happy-ever-after with him. It had always been doomed to end in tears.

It was her own fault for forgetting what was really important. Noah needed a father, and she should have been thinking about finding a family for him, not about Lewis's mouth and Lewis's hands and how they felt against her skin.

Well, now she had a chance to put that right. Rory was Noah's father, and he seemed keen to bond with his small son. She could build a future with him in a way she would never have been able to do with Lewis. Hadn't she told Lewis that successful relationships were about friendship, not passion? Martha slammed the lid of her case down and snapped the locks. She had believed it before, and she would believe it again. She was a pragmatist, not a romantic. It was time to put this infatuation with Lewis behind her and get on with real life again

But first she had to say goodbye to Viola. Lewis's niece was in a sunny mood and at her most charming. She was irresistible when she was like this, thought Martha, her throat tightening. Viola gurgled up at her, played with her toes, flirted with her lashes…she might almost have known that Martha was thinking about leaving her and doing her damnedest to make it as hard as she could.

And succeeding. Martha set her jaw and concentrated on not crying as she changed Viola's nappy for the last time. She didn't want to upset her, but when the taxi came, and Viola realised that Martha was taking Noah but leaving her behind, her small face crumpled with distress and she started to wail.

It was a struggle for Eloise to hold her. 'You should stay,' she told Martha tearfully. 'You belong here.'

Martha's throat was so tight she could hardly speak. 'I can't,' she whispered in a broken voice, that wonderful, invigorating anger swept away in a tidal wave of misery.

'I don't understand why you're leaving,' said Eloise, shaking her head.

Martha didn't understand either by then. She just knew that Lewis had said that he didn't need her.

The tears were pouring down her face as she tried to kiss Viola goodbye, but the baby twisted her head away and hit out at her furiously. It was all she deserved for making such a mess of things, thought Martha desolately, aware that Noah was getting upset as well.

'I'll come back and see you,' she promised, but Viola couldn't understand.

Eloise was crying too by now. 'Better go quickly,' she said.

Rory couldn't understand why Martha was so upset. 'She'll be fine,' he said heartily when she tried to explain how hard it had been to say goodbye. 'Babies don't know who's looking after them, do they?'

Five minutes as a father and suddenly he was an expert on babies. Martha was too tired and dispirited to correct him, but she tried to whip up some enthusiasm as Rory showed her proudly round the project house.

'What do you think?' he asked.

Martha thought it was horrible. It was a small square house, basically furnished, with a fridge full of beer and not much else. The members of the project seemed to use it as a dump more than a base. The scrubby garden was full of empty bottles and broken diving gear, and the living area was piled high with computer printouts, sample jars, crisp packets, squeezed cans of drink, and back copies of scientific journals. There was no shade and the air-conditioning rattled monotonously.

Heartsick, Martha hugged Noah as she looked around her. No deep verandah, no slow *thwock* of ceiling fans, no lagoon at the end of the garden. And, worse, no Eloise, no Viola. No Lewis.

But she had a family. Almost. Maybe.

'This is my room.' Rory opened a door into a room so messy that it made the rest of the house look as if it were the object of obsessive housekeeping. Kicking clothes out of the way, he sat down on the bed and patted it invitingly. 'So, shall we take up where we left off?'

He smiled at her and Martha marvelled at herself. He was gorgeous, blond, smiling, a hunk of manhood oozing sex appeal, and he wanted her, with her crow's-feet and her stretch marks. She should be turning handsprings with gratitude, but she felt absolutely nothing.

'I don't think that's a good idea,' she said, staying by the door. 'Not yet, anyway,' she added as his face dropped. Who knew? She might decide that a younger man with warm blue eyes and the body of a god was preferable to an uptight, middle-aged engineer.

'I just think it would be better if we got to know each other again before we sleep together,' she tried to explain.

'We didn't know each other before,' Rory pointed out with just a trace of sullenness.

It was a fair point. Martha sighed a little. 'It was different then,' was all she could say. She wished Rory wasn't reminding her of a sulky little boy who'd just had his lollipop taken away.

'Noah will probably wake up in the night,' she said, aware that she was trying to placate him and exasperated with herself for doing it. 'I think I'd better sleep with him until he's settled. By then we'll be used to each other again and…well, we'll see.'

It was a sensible enough plan, but as a start to a future which would hopefully give Noah the stability of a secure family background it sounded a little lacking in joy. Martha's mind veered dangerously to the long nights she had spent with Lewis—uptight, middle-aged engineer that he was—and then away again. This wasn't about rocketing passion or the slow burn of desire. This was about building a family for Noah. It was *about* being sensible, not joyful.

In the event, her prediction that Noah would be unsettled that night proved to be well-founded. He cried and cried, and Martha, tired and miserable and very close to the edge, wished she could do the same. She missed the house by the lagoon. She missed Viola, and she missed Lewis with a physical ache.

She did her best to comfort Noah and keep him quiet, but the walls were very thin, and they might as well have been sharing a room for all the noise that Rory was spared. He was looking distinctly frazzled by the morning.

'I guess that's what comes with being a father,' he said bravely.

'I'm afraid so,' said Martha, thinking privately that what came with being a father was taking it in turns to get up in the middle of the night. Even Lewis, Mr I'm-never-going-to-be-a-father himself, would get up sometimes to settle Viola or Noah to give her a break…

But she wasn't supposed to be thinking about Lewis, was she?

She smiled brightly. 'Shall I cook something nice for tonight?'

Rory didn't think much of that suggestion. Martha gathered that what little money he had was kept for beer, and that the project members lived off chips and dips while they were in town. A quick look through the kitchen cupboards revealed very little in the way of kitchen equipment, so perhaps that was the only sensible solution.

Bang went her hope of making herself at home in the kitchen. Martha spent the day tidying instead, but that turned out to be a *big* mistake. Rory was horrified when he came home. 'What have you done?' he demanded, looking around him at the immaculate house in dismay. 'We'll never be able to find anything now!'

He recovered his temper in the shower, and apologised to Martha afterwards. 'I'm sorry. I just had a bad day,' he said. 'I don't know what was wrong with that Lewis guy, but he was on my case all day. I couldn't do anything right.' He smiled ruefully at her. 'Let's go out and have a drink.'

Martha had to point out that it was Noah's bedtime, and that they had no babysitter.

'Oh. Right.'

To do him justice, Rory made a quick recovery and spent some time playing with Noah before his bath, but Martha could tell that he was quickly bored. When Noah was in bed they sat in the uncomfortable living area, with its single, harsh overhead light, and made polite conversation over the noise of the air-conditioning.

He's a nice guy, Martha reminded herself. He's intelligent and good-looking and fun and Noah's father. He'd be kind to me and we'd get on, and sex wouldn't be a problem. At least we know that we're compatible in bed. Or we were.

So why do I feel as if I've caught the wrong train and am hurtling in the wrong direction?

She knew why. Rory wasn't Lewis.

Martha could hear Viola crying as she shifted Noah on to her other hip and knocked on the door.

There was a long pause, then Lewis yanked the door open abruptly. 'Yes?' he snapped, before he realised who was standing there, and then he stopped in utter disbelief.

He had Viola, clumsily wrapped in a towel, under one arm. She was still yelling her head off, and he was looking wet and harassed, but to Martha they both looked wonderful. Just seeing them sent a great whoosh of joy and relief through her, depriving her of breath so that all she could do was smile.

Noah, recognising Lewis, and no doubt the sound of Viola's voice, took his thumb out of his mouth and beamed too.

'Martha!' Lewis took an involuntary step towards her and the blaze of expression on his face told Martha all that she needed to know. It was quickly masked, but she had seen. He could pretend all he liked; she wouldn't believe that he wasn't pleased to see her now.

'Shall we swop?' she suggested serenely.

She held out Noah to him, and Lewis was so taken aback that he found himself passing over Viola. The exchange of babies brought them close together, and the scent of her hair made him light-headed. He wanted to clutch her to him to make sure that she was real, but she was already stepping back, murmuring to Viola, who was piggy-eyed with crying and hiccuping disconsolately into Martha's neck, comforted already by her familiar smell.

'Come on, let's get you dried,' Martha said to her, and headed calmly towards the bathroom.

Lost for words, Lewis stared after her for a moment, before he turned his gaze to the stuff that the taxi driver had unloaded on to the verandah, and lastly to Noah. The baby smiled and bumped his forehead against him in greeting and Lewis felt something hard and tight inside him dissolve as he found himself smiling back.

'Welcome back,' he said to Noah. 'It's good to see you again.'

Following Martha to the bathroom, he found her expertly dusting Viola with baby powder. 'Martha, what's going on?' he said in an effort to sound in control. 'What are you doing here?'

'I've come to finish my contract,' she said without looking up from the baby.

Lewis closed his eyes briefly. It was so much what he had wanted to hear that he was afraid he might be imagining things, and that this would all turn out to be a dream, but when he opened them again Martha was still there.

'What about Rory?' he asked, finding his voice at last.

Her hands stilled for a moment, and she glanced at him with one of her clear, direct looks. 'I made a mistake,' she said. 'I'd convinced myself that what Noah needed more than anything was a father, and that the best thing for him would be to grow up in a proper family, but what's the point of a family if it's not a happy one?'

Without waiting for his answer, she turned her attention back to the baby. She fastened the nappy with deft hands and put Viola into a Babygro with an ease that Lewis could only marvel at. When he had tried the two previous nights it had taken him ages as he struggled to keep Viola still and she wriggled and fought and bellowed objections. Martha made it look as if it was the simplest thing in the world.

'I've done a lot of thinking over the last couple of days,' she went on, lifting Viola against her shoulder and cuddling her warm little body, 'and I've changed my mind.'

She turned to face Lewis squarely. 'Now I think that all Noah really needs is for his parents to be happy. It doesn't matter whether we're together or apart, as long as Noah senses that we're doing what we want to do and are with the person we want to be with.

'Rory wouldn't be happy if he's forced into responsibility before he's ready for it,' she said. 'He'll be a better father to Noah for not feeling tied down now. Have you got some milk for her?'

Lewis blinked at the abrupt change of subject, but recovered quickly enough. 'In the kitchen.'

Still gripped by a feeling of unreality, he divided the milk between two bottles and they sat at either end of the sofa with a baby each.

'What did you say to Rory?' he asked Martha when Noah and Viola were guzzling contentedly.

'I told him that it wasn't going to work,' she said, adjusting Noah's bottle slightly as he clutched at it with greedy little hands. 'I told him that nothing would change the fact that he would always be Noah's father, and that I hoped that he would keep in touch so that Noah could get to know him as he's growing up. I said that it would be better for all of us if we didn't try and pretend that we belonged together when we don't, so I was leaving.'

For the first time Lewis felt a twinge of sympathy for Rory. He knew what it was like when Martha said that she was leaving. 'How did he react?'

'I think he was more relieved than anything,' said Martha reflectively. 'He was prepared to have a go, but even after a few days he realized that Noah and I just didn't fit into his life. He's not ready for commitment. He feels that he would be a better father if we weren't together.' She went on with a sideways glance under her lashes at Lewis, 'But he did say that he would come and see Noah when he can.'

Lewis shifted Viola up his arm. 'Where does that leave you?' he asked.

'It leaves me trying to be happy myself.'

'And how are you going to do that?'

'Well,' said Martha, 'I was hoping that you would give me my job back, for a start.'

'Even though that would mean working for someone who's arrogant and selfish and stupid?'

She looked at him with a half-smile. 'You know I don't really think you're stupid, Lewis.'

But arrogant and selfish were still OK, apparently? 'Gee, thanks!' he said ironically.

'I missed Viola,' Martha explained, lifting Noah to rub his back until he burped. 'So did Noah. The days were much too quiet without her. We decided it was worth putting up with you for her, didn't we?' she asked Noah, who gurgled back at her.

She was smiling at her baby and Lewis eyed her, uncertain how much she was joking, until she glanced at him and the gleam of laughter in her brown eyes let him release the breath that he hadn't even been aware that he was holding.

No more was said until Noah's cot had been set up and both babies were settled for sleep, but it was as if everything important had already been said. Martha and Lewis moved easily together, aware that there was no rush, until at last they were able to sit back on the verandah in the dark.

Martha breathed in the scents of night. She could hear the familiar rasp of the insects and the hot wind soughing through the palms, their rustling leaves drowning out the sound of the sea. Beside her, Lewis was solid, real, close enough to touch. She remembered the look on his face when he saw her, and leant back in her chair, closing her eyes with a sigh of pleasure. She had only been away three days, but it felt as if she had been on a long journey and had only just made it home.

'So you came back for Viola?' asked Lewis.

'Partly.' She smiled at his fishing without opening her eyes.

'And?' he prompted her.

Martha lifted her lashes at that, and looked at the bougainvillaea scrambling along the verandah roof. 'And because I was happier here than I've ever been anywhere else,' she said quietly. 'I was never going to be really happy with Rory. He's great, but he's not...' she turned her head to look directly at Lewis '...he's not you.'

There, she had said it. She let out a long breath.

There was a long, long pause. 'You came back for me?'

said Lewis in such a peculiar voice that all at once Martha lost her nerve. Had she been wrong about that expression, after all?

'I know it won't be for ever,' she hastened to reassure him. 'I know you don't want a family. That's OK,' she said. 'I just thought that we could have another couple of months together. We had a good time before, didn't we?'

'Yes,' agreed Lewis. 'We did.'

'I'm not asking for any more than that,' said Martha. 'Just two months, being the way we were before. No commitments, no creeping domesticity...just the two of us.'

'And Viola and Noah,' he pointed out. 'They're commitments, aren't they?'

She looked at him, a little confused. 'Of course they are, but I was thinking about the evenings, after they're in bed. It would just be the two of us then. I'm not talking about for ever, Lewis. I'm talking about now.'

'And would that really be enough to make you happy? Two months, and then goodbye?'

Martha swallowed. 'I would be happier than I would be if I wasn't here with you,' she told him.

'Why?' asked Lewis softly, and her mouth dried.

'You know why.'

'I want you to say it.' He held out his hand. 'Come here,' he said, and tugged her gently on to his lap. 'Say it,' he said.

'I love you,' said Martha. It was easier to say than she had thought. She slid her arms around his neck and said it again. 'I love you. I need you. I've missed you.'

Lewis smiled and ran his hand down her spine, sending a delicious shiver of anticipation through her. 'Say it again.'

'I love you. I love you,' she said obediently, punctuating her words with little kisses, a blizzard of them, all along his jaw from his ear to the edge of his mouth. 'I love you.'

His smile deepened, but still he held back tantalisingly. 'Is this love as in companionship and respect?'

'No, it's love as in passion and desire and wanting you more than I've ever wanted anyone before,' Martha murmured. 'I've changed my mind about love.'

'Ah,' said Lewis, pulling her closer. 'You don't think it's about practicality any more?'

'No.' She nestled into him, pressing her face into his throat, breathing in the scent of him, touching her lips to his skin. 'I think it's about not feeling complete without you,' she whispered against his jaw. 'It's about the world being out of kilter when you're not there. It's about that feeling of coming home when you hold me like this.'

'That is a change,' he agreed, and the undercurrent of laughter in his voice warmed her.

'It's about feeling as if the sun's come out whenever you smile. About the way you only have to touch me and I'm on fire. About lying next to you and feeling that my heart is going to burst with loving you.'

'In that case,' said Lewis, 'I think I must love you too.'

Martha straightened abruptly. 'Really?'

'Well, don't sound so surprised!' He pretended to sound offended, and then his smile faded and his face was very serious as he smoothed the hair away from her face and held her between his palms. 'I missed you,' he said softly. 'When you left…' He trailed off. 'I can't tell you how I felt then. It was as if someone had switched off all the lights, and then tonight, when I opened the door and there you were, and suddenly they were all blazing again.'

'That's very poetic for an engineer,' she teased him.

'It's true,' said Lewis. He searched her face with his eyes. 'I do love you, Martha. I love you more than you'll ever know.'

And then, at last, he kissed her. Martha melted into him, giving herself up to the heady pleasure of being able to kiss him back, to touch him and taste him and hold him. She pressed herself against him as they kissed, long, deep, delicious kisses, while the knowledge that he loved her lit a glow deep inside her. It seeped outwards, to her fingertips and the ends of her lashes and out through her pores, until she was incandescent with happiness, radiating it so intensely that she half expected to see her skin luminous in the darkness.

'You know,' murmured Lewis after a while, 'there's still one or two things that we should clear up.'

'Later,' whispered Martha against his mouth. She didn't want to clear anything up. She didn't want to stop, and she didn't want to talk. She just wanted to touch him more, kiss him more, feel him more...

'Later,' Lewis agreed raggedly, and tipped her off his lap to pull her ungently to his room where they fell together on to the bed and forgot about anything but each other.

It was a very long time before they got round to clearing anything up. They lay tangled together, boneless and breathless with delight, still savouring the magic they had created between them.

'Is this you trying to soft-soap me into giving you your job back?' Lewis asked lazily as her hand drifted possessively over his chest.

Martha laughed and turned to press a kiss into his warm shoulder. 'Is it working?'

'Well, I don't know,' he said, pretending to consider. 'There's a bit of a problem.'

'What sort of problem?' She smiled as her hand slid lower.

'Stop that,' said Lewis, but without much conviction. 'The thing is, I'm not sure if I can give you your job back at all—or at least not under the same terms.'

Martha paused. 'You're not serious?'

'I am, I'm afraid. I'm not going to need a nanny any more.'

'Oh.' Taking her hand away, she lay back down beside him. 'Oh, I see.' That was a lie, for a start.

'I talked to Savannah today,' Lewis began to explain. 'She's out of the clinic and raring to start a new life.'

'Well…that's good…' Martha forced herself to sound more enthusiastic. 'Good, I'm pleased.' Another lie. She didn't feel pleased at all. She felt jealous. She'd just got Viola back and she didn't want to lose her again, but how could she say that? Savannah was Viola's mother.

She drew a breath. 'When is she coming to get Viola?'

'She's not.' Under even fewer illusions about his sister, Lewis's voice was very dry. 'She was full of some man she'd met in the clinic. It turns out that he's something in television. He's convinced her that she has a great future as a chat show hostess, of all things, and he wants to take her to the States. Savannah thinks that Viola might complicate things,' he finished.

It was all Martha could do to bite back her opinion of a mother who could think of her baby as a complication, but in the event she might as well not have bothered.

'I know,' said Lewis, exactly as if she had spoken. 'She wanted me to keep Viola for another six months.'

'And you said no?'

'No, I told her that she can't pick up Viola and drop her whenever it suits her. Of course she'll always be Viola's mother, and she can jet in and out as often as she wants, but if Viola stays, she stays permanently. She needs the security of knowing that whatever her mother is doing her home will always be with me.'

'What did Savannah say to that?' asked Martha, knowing how she would have reacted if anyone had proposed bringing up Noah for her.

'She thought it was a wonderful idea,' said Lewis. He

looked at her out of the corner of his eye and a smile touched the corners of his mouth. 'She's not like you.'

'But doesn't she know how you feel about families?'

'Ah, but you see I've changed my mind too.' He rolled over to lean up on one elbow and smooth a strand of hair from her face with such tenderness that Martha's heart cracked.

'The trouble is,' he said, 'I've got used to having a family now, and when you and Noah left I realised that I couldn't go back to living on my own, even if I'd wanted to. I'm sure I'd get more work done, but I wouldn't feel so alive, and the house would be empty and I would be all on my own. I don't want that any more.'

Lovingly, his fingers traced the line of her cheek. 'It wasn't a home any more when you were gone. Viola hated it, and so did I. We needed you and Noah to come back, and now that you have everything feels right again.'

Martha smiled and slipped her arms around him. 'I still don't see what the problem is,' she confessed. 'If Viola is going to be a permanent part of your life, then you're going to need a nanny more than ever, aren't you?'

'No.' Lewis shook his head definitely. 'I don't need a nanny. I need you. I need you to make wherever we are a home, and nannies don't do that. I've got to know that you're going to stay for a lot longer than a couple of months.'

'That shouldn't be a problem,' she said. 'How long were you thinking of?'

'A very long time,' he said firmly.

'How long is very long?'

He pretended to consider. 'I'm not sure that I'm prepared to settle for anything less than for ever.'

'I think I could do that,' said Martha.

'Thinking isn't good enough,' he said. 'You've got to be sure.'

'I am sure,' she said. 'I'm surer than I've been about anything else in my life,' she told him, and drew his head down for a long, sweet kiss of promise.

'For ever it is, then,' said Lewis contentedly when he lifted his head at last.

'I hope you're going to make it worth my while,' she teased. 'I'm used to a salary, you know.'

'It's not really economical to keep paying you a salary,' he pointed out, straight-faced, as she stretched luxuriously beneath his hands. 'I was thinking more of marrying you and saving on that particular cost.'

Martha managed a mock pout. 'That's all very well, but what would I get out of it?'

'You'd get me, you'd get Viola.' Lewis ticked off the advantages on his fingers. 'You'd get a family for Noah, and you'd get to be loved and needed by all of us.' His smile faded as he looked down into her dark, shining eyes. 'What do you say?'

'I couldn't ask for anything more,' she said honestly.

'Do I take that as a "yes", then?'

'That really depends on what the question was,' she pointed out, and he drew her closer.

'If the question was "Will you marry me?"…'

Martha heaved a blissful sigh. 'Then my answer would definitely be "yes"!'

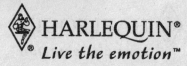

The world's bestselling romance series.

HARLEQUIN®
Presents

Seduction and Passion Guaranteed!

OUTBACK KNIGHTS
Marriage is their mission!

From bad boys—to powerful,
passionate protectors!

Three tycoons from the Outback
rescue their brides-to-be....

**Coming soon in Harlequin Presents:
Emma Darcy's exciting new trilogy**

Meet Ric, Mitch and Johnny—once three Outback bad
boys, now rich and powerful men. But these sexy city
tycoons must return to the Outback to face a new
challenge: claiming their women as their brides!

**MAY 2004: THE OUTBACK MARRIAGE RANSOM #2391
JULY 2004: THE OUTBACK WEDDING TAKEOVER #2403
NOVEMBER 2004: THE OUTBACK BRIDAL RESCUE #2427**

"Emma Darcy delivers a spicy love story...
a fiery conflict and a hot sensuality."
—*Romantic Times*

Available wherever Harlequin books are sold.

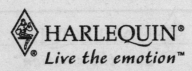

HARLEQUIN®
Live the emotion™

Visit us at www.eHarlequin.com

HPEDARCY

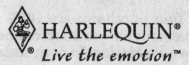

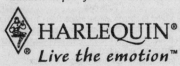